"He looks like he lives up to the Thoroughbred's reputation— hot-blooded," Lora Leigh murmured.

Flint tensed, his own blood heating as he watched her. The transformation from ice queen when she looked at him to soft lines of pleasure on her face as she studied the horses intrigued him.

He suddenly itched to have her look at him with that same softness, with admiration, but quickly tamped down the thought. Becoming involved with an employee was strictly against his rules.

Flint nodded. "The feisty, independent ones are the most challenging but the most rewarding."

Her gaze swung to his, and her eyes flickered with some indefinable emotion. He longed to break all the rules and kiss her. No matter the consequences.

Dear Reader,

I've been writing for Harlequin Intrigue since 1998 and love the wonderful romantic suspense stories and amazingly talented authors of this genre.

When I was asked to collaborate with three of these authors to create this miniseries in celebration of Harlequin's 60th anniversary, I jumped at the chance. Although plotting murder with other authors offers its challenges, especially when you live in various parts of the world, it's an exciting adventure.

How did we do it?

We started with the idea of four heroes—a cowboy, sheik, shipping tycoon and prince. The first question was—how could we tie them together?

Once the idea of horse breeding was born, we all tossed in suggestions and the stories quickly came together.

My story, *Platinum Cowboy,* begins the series with Flint McKade, a self-made billionaire rancher, who suddenly finds his business and life sabotaged. Throw in a female veterinarian who comes to work for him with the secret motive of revenge because she believes he cheated her father out of their home, and the sparks automatically fly. Then danger strikes her, and Flint becomes her protector, changing her preconceived images of the sexy cowboy.

After all, who can resist a tall stud in tight jeans and a Stetson?

I fell in love with Flint and his ranch as I wrote the story and I hope you do, too!

And thanks to the DIAMONDS AND DADDIES team of writers for their creativity and flexibility, especially to Ann Voss Peterson for walking me through the ins and outs of a horse breeding operation. Any mistakes are solely mine!

Happy Anniversary, Harlequin!

Rita Herron

RITA HERRON

PLATINUM COWBOY

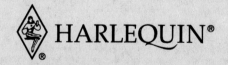

HARLEQUIN®

TORONTO • NEW YORK • LONDON
AMSTERDAM • PARIS • SYDNEY • HAMBURG
STOCKHOLM • ATHENS • TOKYO • MILAN • MADRID
PRAGUE • WARSAW • BUDAPEST • AUCKLAND

To the Diamonds and Daddies team of writers—
you're the greatest!

Recycling programs
for this product may
not exist in your area.

ISBN-13: 978-0-373-69382-5
ISBN-10:   0-373-69382-6

PLATINUM COWBOY

ABOUT THE AUTHOR

Award-winning author Rita Herron wrote her first book when she was twelve, but didn't think real people grew up to be writers. Now she writes so she doesn't have to get a *real* job. A former kindergarten teacher and workshop leader, she traded her storytelling to kids for romance, and writes romantic comedies and romantic suspense. She lives in Georgia with her own romance hero and three kids. She loves to hear from readers so please write her at P.O. Box 921225, Norcross, GA 30092-1225, or visit her Web site at www.ritaherron.com.

Books by Rita Herron

CAST OF CHARACTERS

Flint McKade—A self-made billionaire cowboy who owns Diamondback Ranch. Someone is sabotaging his ranch and determined to destroy him.

Dr. Lora Leigh Whittaker—This veterinarian has a grudge against Flint McKade, and now her younger brother who came to work incognito for McKade is missing.

Johnny Whittaker—Lora Leigh's brother came to Houston to get revenge on Flint McKade—where is he now?

Tate Nettleton—Flint's half brother hates that Flint is successful and feels Flint owes him.

Lawrence MacIroy—He's bitter because Flint bought the prized stallion Diamond Daddy out from under him. Would he kill to get him back?

Howard Reed—A vindictive rancher who is suing Flint because he feels Flint cheated him out of his property.

Sylvester Robbins—He's in charge of transporting the horses from the auction house to Flint's ranch—does he know more about the sabotage than he's telling?

Roy Parkman—A ranch hand who died from the same strange flu outbreak that has made two of Flint's horses ill—did he have something to do with the virus?

Amal Jabar—The Middle Eastern contact Flint deals with when importing the Arabian horses—could he be involved in some kind of smuggling ring?

Rueben Simms—The pilot who died bringing the Arabians into the Houston airport—was he involved in the plan to sabotage Flint?

Brody Green—The cop investigating the airport murders and the sabotage at the Diamondback Ranch—does he have his own ax to grind with Flint?

Deke Norton—He's a friend and colleague who offers advice to the Aggie four team—is he as trustworthy as he seems?

Akeem Abdul, Jackson Champion and Viktor Romanov—Flint's closest friends, members of the Aggie Four.

Chapter One

His best friend, Prince Viktor Romanov, and the entire royal family had been killed.

Grief welled in Flint McKade's chest as he strode through the atrium to the airport bar to meet his friends and business associates, Jackson Champion and Akeem Abdul.

Flint's Aggie Ring winked beneath the fluorescent lights, reminding him of their college days at Texas A&M and that the four men had called themselves the Aggie Four.

But now one of them was gone.

Emotions clogged Flint's throat. How could they be the Aggie Four with only three men? It wasn't right....

And to think that when he'd first met Viktor, he'd scoffed at his title. Hell, he'd been a poor cowboy with a bad attitude and a chip on his shoulder, a kid who'd grown up with no chance for a future.

Unless he made it himself.

A cowboy and prince as friends—never.

After all, he'd never lived anywhere but on the ranch

where his parents worked. Viktor had grown up as a middle-class boy in London and had gone to schools all over the world. His entire family had been exiled from their country, Rasnovia. So Viktor had gone to school on scholarships, with the goal of giving his life to his country.

That had impressed the hell out of Flint. Seeing Viktor so determined had inspired Flint to believe that he could accomplish big goals himself. Then he'd learned that Viktor had lost his father when he was a teen, and they'd bonded over shared grief.

Viktor had introduced him to Akeem, a sheik from Beharrian, and another unlikely friendship had formed. In their fraternity, their tight-knit brotherhood had spread to encompass Jackson, sealing the Aggie Four.

Each of them had had to overcome almost insurmountable obstacles to achieve success. But they were driven, ambitious and determined.

Instead of future business leaders of America, they'd vowed to become future billionaires. *Self-made* billionaires.

And each had succeeded.

Once they'd built their financial empires, they'd decided to give back by creating a nonprofit foundation to raise money for charities.

Flint spotted his friends' dejected faces as they sat slumped at a bar table, a pitcher of beer untouched in front of them, with three mugs waiting.

Three, not four.

One member of their brotherhood was missing.

Killed, of all times and places, in a violent explosion at the palace on Rasnovian Independence Day.

Sweat trickled down his jaw. It couldn't be true. It couldn't have happened.

Akeem caught his eye as he approached, the devastation on his face mirroring Flint's. They were supposed to be celebrating their latest venture tonight, not mourning Viktor's death. Although Flint's five-hundred-acre ranch bred and trained thoroughbreds, quarter horses and beef cattle, Akeem had convinced him to try his hand at Arabians, and he was expecting the shipment within the hour. Jackson's company Champion Enterprises had handled the arrangements.

Flint always met his shipments in person.

He claimed a chair across from Akeem, with Jackson on his right. In the midst of the crowded airport terminal, the strained silence grew tense. No one wanted to speak.

Saying the words out loud would make it all too real.

Flint lifted the pitcher and filled the three mugs, then watched the head on the beer fizzle as he contemplated what to say.

"I can't believe it," he finally said.

Akeem scraped his hand over his chin. "The country isn't releasing any details."

"Do you think the rebels in Rasnovia killed the royal family?" Jackson asked in a gravelly voice.

Flint shrugged. "That would be my guess. Once the democracy was established, the royal family had intended to stay on as ambassadors."

Viktor had been an icon to his country; he'd worked

diligently to repair Rasnovia's infrastructure and jump-start its economy.

The Aggie Four had also invested in Rasnovia's businesses. But money wasn't the issue tonight. Their friend's death was all that mattered.

Flint raised his mug to toast their departed buddy, and Jackson and Akeem followed, but then Flint's cell phone trilled.

His pilot. He connected the call, frowning at the sound of static popping over the line.

"Reuben?"

"T-trouble," Reuben said in a choked voice. "Help...."

Flint's heart pounded, and he lurched up. "I'll be right there."

"What is it?" Jackson asked.

"Something's wrong. Let's go." He tossed some cash on the table to pay for the beer; then the three of them raced toward security.

Joey Stamos, the chief of security, met them at the gate and transported them to the plane, which had already taxied up to the loading dock. The runway lights had been cut as well as the exterior lights, pitching the plane into total darkness.

"What the hell is happening?" Jackson muttered.

"You think someone's trying to steal the Arabians?" Akeem asked.

Flint cursed. "Over my dead body."

Suddenly all hell broke loose, and gunfire exploded outside. The security guards at the loading dock scurried into action, crouching down as they surrounded the plane.

"Stay down and inside!" Stamos ordered as he slid from the vehicle.

Flint reached for the door handle, but Stamos grabbed his arm. "I mean it, McKade. Those are automatic weapons."

Dammit, Stamos was right. He hadn't exactly come packing to the airport.

Another round of bullets pinged back and forth. The guards exchanged fire, their bullets pelting metal, dust flying, for what seemed like hours as Flint and his friends waited.

Finally, things settled down, and Stamos returned. "It's clear, but not good."

Flint imagined the worst as he climbed out of the vehicle. "I have to see."

Stamos put a hand to his chest to stop him. "No, wait on CSI."

"Stamos, those are my people in there," Flint growled. "And I have to check the Arabians."

Stamos finally nodded but ordered Jackson and Akeem to remain behind and wait for the local police and forensic team.

Fear and anger gnawed at Flint as he followed Stamos to the plane and climbed on board.

The moment he stepped up to the cockpit, the coppery scent of blood assaulted him. Then he glanced inside, and his chest clenched at the sight of the bloody massacre. His pilot had been shot in the head at close range, his blood and brain matter splattered across the instrument panel.

He spun around, fury churning through him, then

spotted two ranch hands sprawled on the floor, dead in the galley. One was an older guy he'd known for years. The other was a young man, but his face had been shattered during the massacre and was unrecognizable. Multiple gunshot wounds marked their chests and limbs, their blood running like a river down the aisle.

Choking back bile, he sidestepped the bodies and rushed to the stalls to check the horses.

Normally sedated, now they were kicking and whinnying madly, the small plane rocking with the force.

"Shh, guys. It's over." He gently soothed the animals, scrutinizing each one for injuries, but thankfully, they appeared to be unharmed.

"We got the shooters," Stamos said as he came up behind Flint. "There were two, both with heavy artillery."

Flint's jaw tightened. "I want to question them."

Stamos shook his head. "Too late. They're dead."

Flint fisted his hands, wanting to pound something. A dozen questions raced through his head. Questions the cops would ask. Questions he wanted the answers to himself.

Who were the shooters? Had they been working alone, or had someone else orchestrated this attack?

"Looks like someone either wanted the horses or wanted to hurt your business," Stamos said quietly.

Flint nodded. Damn right, they had. And he'd find out who had endangered his Arabians and killed his men.

Then the SOBs would pay.

DR. LORA LEIGH WHITTAKER hated Flint McKade.

Yet here she was, driving past the giant live oaks

flanking the private road to the Diamondback Ranch—McKade's mega-conglomerate *estate*—to work for him. He'd named the huge operation after his prized stallion, Diamondback Jack, a thoroughbred that had won him millions in races and stud fees, and not, as she'd first thought, after the diamondback rattlers so prominent on the rugged Texan land.

Bitterness swelled inside her. He was a snake himself. Always coiled and ready to strike and take advantage of the small-time ranchers.

She had to suck up her pride and hatred, though, because she needed answers.

Her younger brother, Johnny, was missing.

The last time she'd spoken to him, he'd been working incognito on the Diamondback.

No matter how brilliant McKade seemed through the lens of the press, she was convinced he'd made his money by cheating small-time ranchers and farmers out of their homes and property and built his empire like some sort of shrine to himself. He probably had a gargantuan ego to match that fat bank account of his, too.

She'd read the business sections, the numerous features of him in various magazines and newspapers, and knew he was worth at least a billion.

And to think what he'd bought her father out for.

No amount of money would have been enough. The Double W had been their home, her parents' dream. They'd poured blood, sweat and tears into the place, their entire life and soul into farming and ranching, and had raised her and Johnny to love the land as they did.

It was the only place Lora Leigh had ever called

home. The place where she'd run and played with Johnny when she was little. Where she'd gotten her first horse, Miss Whinny, where she'd learned to ride and developed her love of animals. Where she'd decided she wanted to be a veterinarian.

In the house on that ranch she'd shared cozy Christmases with her family, stringing the tree they'd cut down themselves with popcorn and decorating it with handmade ornaments. There her mother had painted bird feeders for the yard and planted flowers in the spring.

It had killed Lora Leigh to lose her home.

Especially knowing her father had taken out a second mortgage to fund college and vet school for her.

She swiped at the flood of tears streaming down her face, gulping back grief and anger. Two days after her father had sold their home to Flint McKade, he'd killed himself.

All because of McKade. The bastard.

A choked sob tore from her chest, the tendrils of grief clawing at her. Life had taken an even nastier downward spiral then. Johnny had turned to booze and trouble. Even while grieving for her father, she'd tried to drag him up from the bottom of the barrel and convince him to straighten up. She couldn't lose him, too.

But when he'd finally sobered up, his anger had surfaced, and he'd started talking revenge.

Six weeks ago, he'd gone to the Diamondback and landed a job under another name. He thought he could find some dirt on McKade to destroy him, something to prove he had cheated their father out of his land. But she hadn't heard from Johnny in over two weeks, and he always checked in weekly.

What if he'd found something incriminating, and McKade had discovered what he was up to? Would McKade be so ruthless as to get rid of her brother to keep him silent?

Panic threatened, but she tamped it down, tightening her fingers around the steering wheel. If she found out he had, she'd go to the police.

She'd considered it already, but then she'd have to admit that her brother had gone to the Diamondback seeking revenge on McKade. And what if Johnny had done something or planned to do something illegal…?

Her gaze was drawn to the pastureland and the horses galloping in the pens as she neared the Diamondback's main house. Nerves on edge, she parked in the circular drive in front of the house, noting the nearby corrals and bunkhouse, and inhaled a calming breath as she removed her compact to repair her tear-swollen eyes.

She'd wondered if McKade would recognize her name and refuse to hire her because of her father, but she hadn't dealt with him directly or even met him yet.

He probably didn't know half the names of the families he'd destroyed.

Money was obviously the only thing that mattered to him.

Well, family was the only thing that mattered to her. Family and her home.

He had already stolen two of those from her.

If he'd hurt Johnny, he'd be sorry.

"THE ARABIANS ARE SAFE and in quarantine now on my ranch," Flint told Amal Jabar, the Middle Eastern contact who'd arranged for him to import the new breed. "I'm not sure if the attackers wanted to kill my men or steal the horses, but I intend to find out. I'm going to need a list of everyone who works for you, and anyone else who knew about the shipment."

"You're suggesting that one of my people sabotaged the plane?" Amal said, with an angry edge to his voice.

Flint was skating on thin ice here: Akeem had referred him to Amal and trusted the man. "I'm not implying anything," Flint said. "But men died tonight, so we have to investigate every angle."

Amal hesitated. "I'll fax you the list. And I'll also question each one of them myself. If I find anything suspicious, I'll let you know."

"Thanks, Amal. I appreciate it."

"Take good care of the Arabians," Amal said.

"Don't worry. I will."

He hung up, undressed, then climbed in the shower. He closed his eyes as the warm water sluiced over him and the images of the dead men haunted him. Three men had lost their lives on a job for him, which meant their blood was on his hands.

He would find the responsible party if it killed him.

Then the families could have some closure, knowing that the killer had been brought to justice. It was the least he could do for them.

He stumbled from the shower, then dragged on a pair of jeans and a denim shirt, tensing at the sound of the doorbell ringing. The last thing he wanted right now was company.

He wanted to down a stiff drink, to mourn his friend in peace, and to figure out who had attacked his shipment and his men tonight, because they had attacked *him*.

And what if someone came after the Arabians again?

He'd gotten them settled into the quarantine area for the two weeks necessary to run the veterinary tests required under state and federal law. Maybe he should hire extra security.

A knock sounded at his suite door. "Mr. McKade, you have a guest."

Hoping it was the police, with answers, he opened the door and found Lucinda, his housekeeper and cook, staring up at him with swollen eyes. She'd worked for Flint for ten years now and felt more like a mother to him than an employee. He'd asked her repeatedly to call him by his first name, but she refused.

And she had been friends with Grover, the older ranch hand who'd died tonight, and had taken the news badly. "Who is it?"

"Dr. Whittaker."

Oh, hell. He'd forgotten she was supposed to arrive tonight.

"Tell her I'll be right there."

Lucinda nodded and descended the stairs. He buttoned his shirt and ran a hand through his still-damp hair. He'd been dreading this meeting for weeks, ever since her father had committed suicide. He'd been shocked when she'd applied for a job as one of his vets and he'd wondered if she had somehow discovered the truth about the deal he'd made with her father.

Maybe she wanted to thank him for bailing out her father before he lost everything they owned. And then for giving her a job...

Not that she couldn't practice anywhere in the state. He'd read her credentials; she'd graduated top of her class. Besides, she was an Aggie grad as well, and Aggies took care of their own.

He heaved a weary breath and went down the stairs, half expecting her to be short and stubby like her father, a boyish girl who was strong enough to handle the horses.

But his gut clenched when he spotted the woman sitting in his office, in one of his overstuffed leather chairs.

Dear Jesus, she was *nothing* like her old man.

Not stubby or boyish, but petite, and so delicate looking that the chair nearly swallowed her slight frame. *Slight but curvy,* he thought as his gaze landed on her full breasts, which were straining against that damn suit jacket.

Long golden hair brushed her shoulders, shimmering beneath the lamplight like finespun silk, and her skirt showcased a pair of killer legs, with firm calves that could grip a horse—or a man—when riding him. His gaze raked south, to her heels, long, spiky things with pointed toes that made a man's mouth water, made a man imagine having her in bed, wearing nothing but the damn shoes.

She was his new vet?

He swallowed back a knot of hunger that suddenly shot through his body with lightning speed and caught him completely off guard.

She looked up and saw him, then stood, the scent of honey and softness emanating from her. And her cobalt-blue suit was the same rich color as her incredibly big blue eyes.

Eyes that turned icy cold when he extended his hand.

His shoulders stiffened. She obviously hadn't come here to thank him for saving her father's ass.

In fact, judging from her pursed mouth and the brusque handshake she offered, she didn't like him at all.

So why in the hell had she accepted the job on his ranch?

Chapter Two

Lora Leigh's chest tightened as Flint McKade's gigantic palm swallowed hers. She'd seen photographs of him in the newspaper as well as in several magazines—once on the cover, as one of the top ten eligible bachelors in Texas—and had braced herself to remain unaffected by his good looks and his money.

She refused to swoon over a man, especially one who ran roughshod over the working people.

But in spite of her resolve, a sliver of undeniable attraction splintered through her as his dark brown eyes raked over her. He was taller than he looked in his photographs, at least six-two, and had a linebacker's shoulders and a washboard stomach. She knew that from the charity calendar for which he'd posed shirtless. His skin was bronzed from the sun and his shaggy, dark-brown hair brushed his shoulders like a renegade cowboy.

And surprisingly, his hands were calloused.

So the stories were right: he actually did *work* on the ranch himself, and did not just delegate and oversee his minions.

"Dr. Whittaker, it's nice to meet you," he said. "I was sorry to hear about your father."

His comment immediately shattered the moment, jerking her back to her mission.

And the fact that she hated Flint McKade. That she was here to get dirt on him and find her little brother.

She dropped his hand yet refused to reveal her emotions, so she shifted slightly and swallowed the lump in her throat. "Thank you."

He nodded, then gestured for her to sit again, and he claimed the soft leather chair across from her. "Would you like something to drink? Coffee, or something stronger?"

"No, thank you."

He studied her for a moment, and she settled her sweating palms on her legs and inhaled. His big body was taking up all the air in the room.

"I trust my manager worked out the details of your contract," Flint said. "Your salary, benefits, days off."

She nodded, hating to concede that his offer had been more than generous. And she needed the money, dammit. "Yes, that's all settled."

"Housing on the Diamondback is optional," he continued. "If you prefer to commute, that's up to you. But we start early around here, at the crack of dawn."

"Housing on the ranch is fine," Lora Leigh said curtly. "And I'm well aware of how early ranch life starts, Mr. McKade. I grew up on a working one myself, with horses and cattle."

His eyes darkened, narrowing beneath thick dark brows. "Call me Flint, Lora Leigh."

She licked her lips. She didn't want to get personal, and

the way his hoarse, throaty voice murmured her name sounded way too personal. "I'd prefer Mr. McKade."

"I'd prefer Flint." His voice deepened, brooking no argument. "All my employees, including my ranch hands, are on a first-name basis. I consider them part of the Diamondback family."

Unprepared for that comment, she bristled. He had destroyed her family, so thinking of herself as part of his was unacceptable.

"Can I ask you a question, Lora Leigh?"

She stiffened. "Of course."

"Why did you accept the position here?"

A sliver of unease rippled up her spine. Had he discovered that her brother had come there to spy on him?

Did he know that she was here for the same reason?

FLINT COULD BARELY DRAG his eyes away from Lora Leigh as she squirmed under his scrutiny, her efforts at maintaining that cool facade failing miserably at his question. She looked as if she was sinking into quicksand, and he almost wanted to toss her a rope to save her. Instead, he remained focused, intent on waiting her out. If she was going to work for him, he wanted to know she was loyal, especially after today's horrific events.

"Lora Leigh, why did you accept the job on the Diamondback?" he asked again, quietly.

His gut tightened at the way she clamped her teeth over her lower lip. A lip that was going to be bruised if she didn't stop chewing on it.

His hand itched to reach up and soothe the delicate skin with his finger—or his lips.

He silently cursed. He didn't like the way she'd mesmerized him a damn bit. He had enough on his plate right now, dealing with Viktor's death and the sabotage and murder of his employees. He didn't need the distraction of a woman.

Especially one who obviously didn't like him.

The reason intrigued him and pissed him off at the same time. She'd made up her mind about him before they'd even met, no doubt because he'd bought her father's property, and instead of seeing him as a good guy who'd saved her father from financial ruin, she saw him as the enemy.

"You have one of the largest and finest spreads in Texas," she said. "You breed thoroughbreds for racing, with incredible results, as well as quarter horses that have won numerous awards." She gestured at the Triple Crown trophy encased in glass, along with other trophies his quarter horses had earned. Just last year, Salamander won the National Cutting Horse Association Championship. "What veterinarian wouldn't want to work at such a famous and prestigious ranch?"

The ones who wanted their own pieces of the pie. He'd been one of them growing up. His father had been a ranch hand and his mother a cook on another big spread, but Flint had wanted to own his own land. Be his own boss.

Master the business himself, not work for someone else. It was one reason he treated his hands like family.

"You've obviously done your homework," he said, although he wasn't surprised. According to her references, she was smart, motivated, a hard worker who took initiative.

A small smile graced her face, offering him a glimpse of what she might look like if she really smiled.

"Of course. You're even larger in person than in your photos."

He arched a brow at that, noting the way she instantly averted her gaze, as if she hadn't meant to personally comment on his looks.

A dozen different clips of articles that had been printed rolled through his head. Some complimented his skill as a businessman and rancher, especially his innovative breeding techniques and efforts at conservation. Others noted his charity donations, and the hunting regulations and wildlife preservation measures he'd championed.

But there were others that were not so flattering.

Ones that painted him as a conniving, cold son of a bitch who ruthlessly bought out small-time farmers to build his own empire.

And then there was that damn calendar. He didn't know why he'd agreed to pose for the stupid bachelor thing, except that it had raised millions for charity and he liked to give back.

"Well, don't believe everything you read," he murmured.

She folded her hands but refrained from commenting. "I heard you imported some Arabians."

His mouth tightened. "Yes. Then I guess you also heard about the trouble at the airport."

She shook her head and he explained, pure horror mounting on her face. "Are the horses all right?"

Ah, so she did sincerely love horses. She'd do a good job.

Except she was so damn small and delicate. Could she really handle herself?

Only time would tell.

"Thankfully, yes." He checked his watch, then scrubbed a hand over the back of his neck, fatigue wearing on him from the strain of the day.

"I'm anxious to see them, along with the rest of your stock. I watched Diamond Daddy win the derby. What an incredible animal."

He nodded and smiled. "That he is. He's a descendant of Diamondback Jack—"

"The horse you named the ranch after."

He angled his head to study her again. "Right. You obviously researched me."

"Oh, yes. I wanted to be prepared."

He grinned. *Prepared for what? To dislike him?*

Hell, the fact that she did irritated him, but he'd change that. He could be charming when he wanted. Sooner or later, he'd win her over.

And get into her bed.

Don't go there. You have enough to do with breeding season, and with a murderer to catch.

He stood, shaking his head to clear it. "It's too late to show you around tonight. How about we meet in the morning, and I'll give you the grand tour?"

She tensed slightly. "I know you're a busy man, Mr. McKade—"

"Flint."

She sighed. "Flint. One of your ranch hands or managers can give me a tour."

He gritted his teeth. Her attitude was starting to

annoy him. "Nonsense. If you're going to work with my horses, I want to see how they react to you."

She arched a brow. "So this is a test?"

"No, it's just that I can usually judge if an employee is going to click by their interaction with my other workers and with the animals."

Her blue eyes darkened. "And how am I doing so far?"

He grinned. "Let's see how it goes in the morning. Now I'll show you to your quarters."

She stood, brushing down her skirt. "Fine."

He dragged his gaze from her legs and started to tell her to dress for work in the morning, but then he remembered her comment about growing up on a ranch and bit back the gibe. He didn't want to piss her off any more than he already had.

He just hoped she was more endearing to his animals than she was to him.

LORA LEIGH CLIMBED IN her Jeep and followed Flint in his truck down the graveled road, past the most beautiful pastureland she'd ever seen and several barns, to a small white wooden cottage shaded by giant live oaks and elms. A large weeping willow also shadowed the porch with its sweeping, spidery arms, as if to reach out and embrace her.

A swing on the small front porch and a pot of pansies added a homey flair. Dust swirled around her as she parked and climbed out. She went to retrieve her suitcase from the back, but Flint grabbed it and her cosmetic bag, so she retrieved her laptop.

"I have some apartments on the west side and a few

small cottages throughout the ranch for other employees," he said. "But I thought you'd be more comfortable here. It's closer to the barns for the horses you'll be in charge of and will give you some privacy from ranch hands."

She'd read about his housing projects, the apartments both on the ranch and in town.

"Besides the ranch hands, grooms, trainers and their assistants and vets, I have a wildlife biologist on board as well as scientists specializing in crop production. Each of the vets is assigned to a specific area, but I also have a vet clinic near the main house. It has an office and a computer set up and is fully equipped with medical supplies and equipment. It adjoins the office space for my managers." He gestured toward a long white building from which a plume of smoke arose.

"That's the cafeteria. We serve breakfast starting at five o'clock, and meals are available throughout the day." He led her up the narrow pebbled walkway to the porch, then climbed the steps. She couldn't help but notice the way his tight jeans hugged his butt and the way his denim shirt stretched across those massive shoulders.

Heaven help her. She had to stop ogling him. He was the enemy.

Flint unlocked the door and pushed it open, then gestured for her to enter. "It's not fancy, but it's comfortable," he said as she entered.

"It's fine," she said, although it was more than fine. A comfortable oversize blue sofa and a chair sat in the living room, in front of a braided rug, and the area opened to a modern kitchen with a breakfast bar and a pine table.

"It's just one bedroom," he said, "but there's a nice bath, and the view's not bad. You can see the sunrise from the porch in the mornings. The kitchen is stocked with basics to get you started. You're welcome to take meals at the cafeteria, or you can eat on your own."

She enjoyed cooking, and when she closed her eyes, she could still smell the scent of her mother's home-made cinnamon rolls and buttermilk biscuits in the oven and the fresh sausage frying in the pan.

But she intended to use every minute she could here to find out what had happened to Johnny.

Flint strode into the bedroom and settled her suitcase on a luggage rack at the foot of the bed. Two windows, with billowing curtains, flanked the antique four-poster bed, which was covered by a quilt in various shades of blue and white calico.

She stopped to admire the intricate pattern and tiny stitch work. "Oh, my, this is a Dresden plate pattern. Is it handmade?"

He nodded, an odd expression lining his chiseled face. "My mother made it. Quilting was kind of a hobby of hers."

"It's beautiful," she whispered.

He stepped back from the bed, his gaze meeting hers. "Do you quilt?"

She hesitated, reluctant to share anything personal with this man who she was supposed to hate. "Yes. My grandmother and mother were both quilters. They taught me when I was a little girl." And her mother had left her a wedding-ring quilt for her hope chest, the last one she'd made before she died.

Not that Lora Leigh ever planned to marry. She didn't trust men. Some were intimidated by her degree, some thought she was too much of a tomboy, while others implied she wasn't sophisticated enough. She just never seemed to fit....

"Well, I guess we have something in common," Flint said quietly. "Other than our love of horses."

Emotions bounded up to her throat. She didn't want to have anything in common with him. To like him at all.

In fact, she felt like a traitor for being on his land. And especially for thinking for even a moment that Flint McKade was handsome.

That he might not be the bad guy she'd pegged him to be.

No, he was bad. He'd said he was sorry about her father's death, but he hadn't apologized for driving him to suicide. Stealing her father's land had been the last straw.

Flint might as well have put the rifle in her father's hand.

All that blood on the wall...

She couldn't erase the image from her head. Her father's vacant eyes, pale skin, his body covered in blood...

"Well, it's late," Flint said quietly. "I'll let you settle in, and I'll see you in the morning. I'll come by around six."

She didn't trust herself to speak, so she nodded and forced herself not to turn around and watch him leave. But when she heard the door click shut, the tears began to fall.

Wrapping her arms around herself, she walked to the window and looked out into the night. Somewhere in the distance, frogs croaked, a coyote howled and horses whinnied, reminding her of all she loved about ranch life. The land was rugged in places, dotted with rocky areas, boulders, sagebrush and wild animal life, yet crops survived, cattle thrived and breeding season was in full swing. The stars shimmered in the inky night sky like glittering diamonds, the smell of horses and hay and lush green grass welcoming her as if she were home.

But she wasn't home. She'd lost her home because of Flint.

Angrily, she swiped at the tears and cursed herself for being weak and for admiring for even a second the ranch that Flint had built. She'd find out what had happened to Johnny, make sure he was alive and safe; then she'd get the hell off the Diamondback and start over someplace else.

But she'd have to watch herself, force herself to be nice and professional. Flint was so influential in the ranching and farming community; if he wasn't pleased with her work, he could ruin her professional reputation in Texas. And she had no one to take care of her now, no one to turn to, no one to rely on but herself. She had to maintain her reputation and integrity, no matter what.

Of course, if worst came to worst, she could leave the state. Once she found Johnny, there would be nothing holding her here.

She turned to look at the northernmost part of the ranch, at the acreage that had held her home around which swirled the memories that had shaped her life. She had no idea what Flint intended to do with the paltry spread.

But that piece of land would always hold her heart.

And no one would ever touch her heart, especially not Flint McKade.

Chapter Three

The first rays of sunlight streaked the bedroom with various shades of red and orange and gold, waking Lora Leigh from a troubled sleep. She brewed a pot of coffee, then sat in the porch swing to watch the sun slowly rising behind the willow trees, soaking in the quiet as she observed a mare and her foal roaming in the pasture nearby. Others ran across the open space, their manes whipping in the slight breeze. The brilliant colors streaking the horizon made the rolling, lush pastures of the Diamondback look elegant and peaceful, although peace evaded her.

She removed the letter her father had written before he died and unfolded the single piece of plain stationery, studying the scrawled writing. She'd always teased her father about his chicken scratch, but now the narrow print and jagged lines of his penmanship made her long for him even more.

She'd read the suicide note a dozen times, but once again, she reread his last words, needing them to fortify her for the day ahead.

My dearest Lora Leigh,

 I write this to you today with a heavy heart, but I do not want yours to be heavy or for you to mourn me when I'm gone. I have had a wonderful sixty years. I loved your mother with all my heart, and you and Johnny completed my life in a way the ranch couldn't even do.

 The Double W was my dream. The smell of the earth, the feel of soil beneath my hands as I planted crops, the sound of cattle grazing and horses galloping across the land—these were precious to me and reminded me of how fleeting and beautiful life is. I only wish that I could have held on to it for you. But I don't regret a moment of my life or the sacrifices we made as a family together.

 That is what families do.

 As I said, the Double W was my dream. I hope when I'm gone that you both find your own dreams and make them come true. Now it is time for me to join your mother. Don't cry for me. Know that I am with the love of my life, and that we'll both be watching over you.

 I love you always,
 Dad

Lora Leigh wiped at the tears trickling down her cheeks, finished her coffee, then headed to the cafeteria for breakfast, bracing herself to face Flint, take care of his prized animals, and pretend that she didn't despise him for breaking her father's heart.

FLINT READ THE NEWSPAPER over his morning coffee and his breakfast of steak and eggs in his home office. The front page spread about Prince Viktor Romanov's death reminded him of his personal loss. Memories of Aggie tailgating, frat parties, and bonding over beer and chili flashed back.

Dammit, the news reports stated that the bodies of the royal family had been burned beyond recognition. The authorities were still sifting through the debris and bodies from the explosion that had destroyed the palace, trying to make sense of the mess and identify all those lost. But they were convinced that Viktor and his entire family were gone.

Flint scrubbed his hand over his face, his chest aching. But his personal loss was nothing compared to the loss of Viktor's fellow countrymen.

The people of Rasnovia would suffer. In the wake of the political unrest, Viktor had been instrumental in guiding them from Soviet rule to a free and democratic society. The Aggie Four Foundation had invested in the country's infrastructure and burgeoning local busi-nesses, which had improved Rasnovia's economy.

Now the country was in turmoil again, and all the assets would be tied up. And who would bolster Rasnovia's fledgling democracy and protect the people from the rebels?

He finished his coffee, knotting his hand into a fist. He hoped to hell they found the party responsible for the royal family's demise and punished the perpetrators for what they'd done.

Lucinda tottered in, with a smile and more coffee, but

Flint shook his head as his cell phone rang. He checked the number—Norton International. Deke Norton, another Aggie grad, who was a few years older than Flint, Viktor, Jackson and Akeem, had built his empire with a focus on his import/export business and had also offered each member of the Aggie Four financial advice over the years, which had aided them immensely. He was also a good friend and was mourning Viktor's death.

Flint connected the call. "Good morning, Deke."

"Is it?" Deke asked, with an edge to his voice.

Flint pinched the bridge of his nose. "No, not really. I was trying to be optimistic."

"What's going on?" Deke asked. "First Viktor is killed. Then your business is attacked."

Flint frowned. The two couldn't be related. "I know. I still can't believe Viktor is actually gone. I keep expecting him to call and say it was a horrible mistake."

"That's not going to happen," Deke said bleakly. "But what about you? Were you hurt at the airport?"

"No, but two of my ranch hands and my pilot were killed."

"The Arabians weren't injured?"

"They're fine and in quarantine now. I hired a new vet to oversee their medical care. Are you still interested in a purchase?"

"Absolutely. I'll try to get out there soon to take a look. Remember, I get first pick."

"Of course."

"I'm going to the auction house today to look at a few yearlings from promising lines." Deke hesitated. "Do you know if there's going to be a memorial service for

Viktor here in the States? I thought someone at A&M might be planning one."

"I haven't heard, but if I do, I'll let you know." They agreed to talk later, and Flint disconnected the call.

He thanked Lucinda for the meal, stood, grabbed his Stetson and headed toward the door, but his cell phone rang again. He checked the number and saw it was his half brother, Tate Nettleton. Tate was a pain in the ass, and he didn't have time to deal with him now, so he let it ring.

That afternoon he had to attend funerals for Grover and his pilot, but this morning he planned to pick up Lora Leigh and show her around his ranch. Pride bloomed in his chest as he stepped into the warm spring sunshine and inhaled the scent of grass and hay. For a moment, he paused to drink it all in, his land, his horses and cattle, his home. He smiled as he watched two mares gallop across the pasture, their foals trotting awkwardly behind.

He was damn proud of what he'd built here, and for some odd reason, he wanted Lora Leigh to be impressed.

But he sensed she might be immune to his accomplishments.

Although she had liked the handmade quilt he'd had Lucinda dig out from his mother's collection for her bed. Lucinda had questioned him about using items from his treasured personal collection for an employee, but he'd shrugged off her curiosity by saying that it was time he put the quilts to use.

But that wasn't entirely true. He had seen the homemade quilts at the Whittaker house when he'd stopped by to meet with Lora Leigh's father, and he'd decided that using one on the bed in the guesthouse would make her feel at home.

He climbed in his truck, started the engine and drove to the guest cottage, his stomach tightening when he spotted Lora Leigh waiting on the front porch. She was dressed in a baby blue T-shirt that hugged her breasts, jeans that molded her lean, muscular legs and work boots, and she had a jacket tied around her waist. Her beautiful blond hair was tied back in a ponytail, which she'd fitted through the back of an Aggie baseball cap, making her look impossibly young and…sweet.

He'd never seen anyone wear denim the way she did. He'd never thought anything was more beautiful than his horses, but Lora Leigh took his breath away.

But judging from the professional expression tacked on her face as she strode toward him, she didn't think the same about him.

LORA LEIGH SETTLED INTO the passenger seat, trying to ignore the tension simmering between her and Flint as he began the tour. She'd wanted to flash Johnny's picture around the cafeteria this morning and ask about him, but she'd forced herself to wait. She couldn't draw suspicion to herself on the first day at work. She had to be patient, to slowly begin to ask around.

Still, she had searched the sea of faces and had introduced herself to a few ranch hands, assistant trainers and grooms, as well as to two other vets.

Much to her consternation, they had all sung Flint's praises. He was fair. A great boss. He cared about his employees. He offered great benefits and competitive salaries.

He was innovative in farming, cattle ranching and horse breeding, crossing American and European strains in line breeding to develop the ranch's thoroughbreds.

Flint handed her a map of the Diamondback. "Basically, the ranch is divided into four quadrants: northeast, northwest, southeast and southwest. I know that's simplistic, but it works. The northeast and northwest quadrants are the largest and hold the cattle, the southwest quadrant is our agriculture and farming mecca, with fruit groves and wheat our core specialties, and the southeast, where we are now, is designated for horse breeding. We also have race tracks for training."

She nodded and glanced at the map, then at the pastures, barns, stables and small housing areas, as they drove. Live oaks, cedar trees, large pinion pines and elms dotted the property, along with natural shrubs and grass.

"We have about fifty-five thousand cattle in our herd in the north quadrants. The terrain is more mixed, with rugged, high hills, large canyons and valleys with dry creek beds and limestone bluffs. But we get water from the river and also have several running creeks throughout."

"You use helicopters and ATVs for herding?" Lora Leigh asked.

"Yeah, I have the Falcon. But we're still a little old-fashioned around here, and we sometimes work on horseback." He pulled down the lane to a large stable, where she saw two grooms brushing down quarter horses.

"This stable houses the working quarter horses,"

Flint said. "You're welcome to take your pick if you want to ride."

He stopped, and they got out so he could show her inside. A lean-looking cowboy glanced up from where he was organizing tack.

"This is Dr. Whittaker, our new vet," Flint said. "Lora Leigh, this is Jake Kenner. He's new with us, too. A trainer. But if you'll let him know which horse you want to use, one of our hands will have him saddled for you."

Lora Leigh extended her hand. "Nice to meet you, Jake. But I can saddle my own horse."

Flint frowned, but Jake smiled and shook her hand.

From there, Flint showed her the vet clinic and introduced her to Carol, a charming, robust woman in her forties, who served as the office manager. Carol greeted him affectionately.

Flint grinned. "Carol does everything around here. She's in charge of ordering medical supplies, coordinating communication between the veterinarians, shipping medical tests to the lab, arranging for assistants. You know we have interns to check the animals nights and on weekends, to give you time off," he said. "Although we might need you for an emergency."

"Of course," Lora Leigh said. "And I don't mind working weekends."

"Everyone needs a life," Flint said. "I don't want my people burning out."

Darn it. He sounded *nice*. Not what she had expected at all.

Then again, he'd fooled her father into selling him his ranch. That was Flint's game: he knew how to woo and seduce and get what he wanted. She couldn't fall for his act.

Back in the truck, they headed into the horse quadrant. "That's the stud barn, and there's the turnout area for the stallions. The breeding area is part of that barn. We have a separate area for the Thoroughbreds and quarter horses. Broodmares are turned out in pastures, except those getting ready to foal or to be bred." He gestured to some outdoor pens, where she noticed three gorgeous, sleek mares.

"The yearlings are kept separate, and some are being sent to the auction house now. I keep the show horses and sale horses separate as well."

"Do you keep them under lights in the winter to keep their coats slick?"

"Of course." He grinned. "We have some race horses on the road in training, but a couple of our younger ones are kept here near the track."

"You retired Diamond Daddy to stud?" Lora Leigh asked.

"Yes, his first season." Flint smiled again, obviously proud of his prized stallion. "I'm anxious to see if he produces another Triple Crown winner."

"You board and train a lot of horses for Middle Eastern owners?" Lora Leigh asked.

He nodded. "I've got contacts there through my friends. We've raced the quarter horses as well as competed in reining, cutting and roping and in some of the big rodeos."

"I saw that one of yours won the National Cutting Horse Association Championship."

"Yeah. Salamander. We've racked up some quarter horse world championships."

Lora Leigh noticed a bald eagle soaring gracefully above the land. "I heard you've instituted hunting regulations on your land."

"Absolutely. I had to in order to protect the quail and deer. We also have turkeys and whistling ducks. I installed windmills at various intervals and fenced off areas from the cattle to provide water for the wildlife. We have a lot of quail, and we half cut the shrubs to provide shelter for them. We also planted prickly pear cactus plants in open areas to serve as cover for the wildlife."

Impressive. "Have you had any problem with feral pigs?"

He cut her a strange look. "Some. If you spot them, keep back and let me know. And I'd advise you against riding alone in the more isolated areas, especially near the cattle land. Occasionally, we've had trouble with rustlers trying to steal our stock. I'll supply you with a pistol for protection against them and the snakes." He hesitated. "Do you know how to shoot?"

She gave him a sardonic look. "Of course. My father taught me when I was a kid."

He veered to the left and drove to an isolated barn set among ancient trees, a stable and outdoor pens that opened to luscious green pastureland. "This is where we house the Arabians."

Try as she might, she couldn't stop the spurt of excitement budding in her chest. She jumped from the truck before he had a chance to come around to her side and followed him up to the barn, determined to prove herself worthy of her job. Too many men had assumed that due to her size, she wasn't strong or capable enough to handle the magnificent beasts she worked with.

But size had nothing to do with it. She understood the horse's nature, listened to him speak, honed in on his mood and anxieties, and soothed him with her voice and manner.

She reined in her excitement as she entered the barn, knowing the animals would respond to her mood, as she would to theirs and lowered her voice as she approached the stalls.

Four incredible horses had been stalled. Two bays, a chestnut and a gray, which was the largest of the four, standing at least fifteen hands, compared to the average of 14.1 hands of the others.

"What are their names?" she asked.

"The larger bay is Sir Huon, and the other, Lord Myers. The chestnut is Iron Legs, and the gray one, Eastern Promise."

"Nice," she said, stroking Eastern Promise's mane. One of her jobs would be to verify a horse's good disposition before reproducing; another was to meet the quarantine standards and administer medical care.

Iron Legs whinnied and kicked the stall, as if agitated, while Sir Huon stood almost docile. She eased from stall to stall, quietly assessing each horse, noting the refined, angular heads, the large eyes and nostrils, and the small muzzles, searching for any indication that they weren't well bred. But the distinctive concave profiles, the arched necks and structure of the throat-latches looked good, as did the well-angled hips, high tail carriages, and well-laid-back shoulders of the beasts.

"So what do you think?" Flint asked.

She reached out and stroked the taller of the bays. "They're incredible. Of course, I'll conduct some tests, but I think you made a wise choice."

When she angled her head to look at him, he was smiling. "I'm glad you appreciate my animals."

She sucked in a sharp breath, her heart tripping as she met his gaze. Of course she did. The fact that he was a talented, cutting-edge breeder and an intelligent rancher and businessman wasn't in question.

The fact that he cunningly used people to ensure his own personal success was. His choices had driven him to ruin her father and others.

That was why she needed to take him down.

FLINT'S CHEST SWELLED with Lora Leigh's compliment, even though an odd tone tinged her words, as if giving him praise pained her.

But why?

He'd read her résumé and files. She was smart—possibly brilliant—and specialized in equine care.

And she was a horse whisperer. That hadn't been in her file, but it was obvious by the way the animals had quieted the moment she entered the barn. Her quiet, melodic voice had mesmerized them.

As it did him.

Workwise, they would make an incredible team.

But there was definitely an underlying tension between them, a disdain for him, which he couldn't ignore. Besides, he wasn't looking for a partner—just an employee who could complement his staff.

His cell phone trilled, jarring him from his thoughts. The chestnut Arabian whinnied and started to kick at the stall. Flint excused himself and stepped outside to check the phone number. The police.

Maybe they had information about who had sabotaged his shipment and killed his men. "Flint McKade speaking."

"Mr. McKade, this is Detective Brody Green. I'd like to talk to you today."

"Do you have a lead on who attacked my plane?"

"Let's discuss it in person. I'll be at your house at noon. Meet me then."

Flint agreed and hung up, although anxiety knotted his gut. Knowing he had an enemy put him on edge.

He glanced back at the barn, then across his land. Overhead in the distance, he spotted a lone vulture soaring above a copse of trees, its talons bared, as if preparing to swoop down and attack, reminding him that he had a stalker of his own.

Was it possible that one of his own employees had sabotaged him? Had they wanted the Arabians or just to hurt his business?

Who had it in for him? Was it someone he knew and trusted, someone who worked for him or for a competitor?

He mentally ticked down a list.

His half brother, Tate, who hated him because Tate was a leech and Flint had cut him off financially? Lawrence McElroy, because Flint had outbid him for Diamond Daddy? Someone who didn't like his connections to Viktor and the Middle East?

He hated to suspect his own men, people he considered part of his family, but having money meant making enemies, and he obviously had garnered at least one.

He had to figure out who it was before anyone else got hurt.

HE STUDIED THE DIAMONDBACK mansion from his horse. Dammit, how had things gone so wrong at the airport? Nobody was supposed to die that night.

But someone had betrayed him, and that was the cost.

He just hoped to hell that Flint McKade and the police didn't figure out what was going on.

But the murders had attracted the attention of the cops. Not a good sign.

He had to do something to distract them, throw them off the scent.

First, he'd hack into McKade's files, doctor a few things, then sabotage the ranch.

And if anyone interfered, he'd get rid of them, just as he had the men on the plane.

Nothing was going to get in his way now. McKade would go down, one way or the other.

And he'd be laughing as the arrogant bastard fell.

Chapter Four

Flint pocketed the phone, then stepped back inside the barn. Lora Leigh was talking to the chestnut in a soothing voice that he could barely discern. Iron Legs slowly calmed, pressing his nose into her hand as she continued to whisper to him.

Flint hated to interrupt the moment, but he needed to finish the tour and get back to the house before the detective arrived. "Lora Leigh, we should probably move along. I have to meet the police at the house at noon."

She checked her watch and nodded, unable to suppress the faint glow to her cheeks, which hadn't been there before. "Did they find out who tried to sabotage your shipment?"

"The detective didn't say. Maybe he'll tell me more in person." He gestured toward the exit and followed her back to the truck. She had to climb up to get inside, and he almost reached out to give her a lift. But the sight of her tight butt in those jeans made his body twinge, and he knew if he touched her, he might go too far.

Gritting his teeth, he hurried around to the driver's

side, then drove toward one of the race tracks. The truck rumbled over the graveled road. The sun was beginning to heat up as noon approached.

A slight breeze ruffled the trees and stirred the intoxicating scent of the outdoors as he parked in front of the racetrack. "I wanted you to see where we begin training our hopefuls."

A young black quarter horse with white markings on its face trotted inside the arena, its lean body and long legs silhouetted by the brilliant sunshine. A trainer worked with the animal, another led a roan outside and a gray stallion whinnied and bolted away from its trainer inside the paddock.

"He looks like he lives up to the Thoroughbred's reputation, hot-blooded," Lora Leigh murmured.

Flint tensed, his own blood heating as he watched her. The transformation from ice queen when she looked at him to gentlewoman when she studied the horses, intrigued him. She might be small, but she was a natural horsewoman.

He suddenly itched to have her look at him with that same softness, with admiration, but quickly tamped down the thought. He'd given her a job because he felt bad about her father. Becoming involved with an employee was strictly against his rules.

"We just got him, but he's one of our most promising," Flint said.

"He'll be worth the work," Lora Leigh added.

Flint nodded. "The feisty, independent ones are the most challenging but the most rewarding."

Her gaze swung to his, and her eyes flickered with

some indefinable emotion. He wondered if she had grasped his underlying meaning, then chastised himself.

A second ago, he'd latched on to his control.

But in spite of his resolve, she stirred desires he hadn't felt in a long time, including the need to understand a woman, to really know her, not just lose himself between her legs and in her body.

His gaze dropped to her breasts, and his mouth watered.

He had to admit he'd like to do that, too.

"They remind me of the prickly pear," he murmured, unable to tear his gaze from her face. "The flowers are beautiful and exotic." He rubbed the upper part of his backside, with a teasing grin. "But those glochids sting. And they're damn hard to get out."

Lora Leigh laughed, a beautiful musical sound that twisted his insides and made him ache for more. The sun shimmered off her golden-blond ponytail. Her eyes were shaded by the hat, but her lips drew his gaze. Pink, like plump raspberries, they made him want a taste.

Forgetting all reason, he reached out and twirled a strand of her hair that had escaped the clasp between his fingers.

Her laughter died, a sudden passion flamed in her blue eyes, and he leaned forward. Just one taste.

A shadow passed over her face, though, and she shifted and glanced at her watch.

He dropped his hand, feeling like a fool. When she looked back up at him, the ice had returned to her eyes. "You'd better take me back if you're going to meet that detective."

"I'm sorry, Lora Leigh—"

She threw up a hand in warning. "Don't. Let's just keep our relationship on a business level."

Dammit, she was right. He'd made a mistake in touching her.

And it wouldn't happen again.

LORA LEIGH'S HEART POUNDED in her chest as Flint drove her back to the cottage. What was wrong with her? One minute they'd been talking about the horses, and the next he'd cracked that joke about the prickly pear, and she'd imagined him falling on one, the spiny needles sticking in his butt, and she couldn't help but laugh.

Then his eyes had turned hungry.

For a brief second, she'd forgotten who he was and why she was here. That he was her boss, and she despised him. That she'd come here to find Johnny and possibly some dirt on Flint.

But the man had cast some kind of spell over her, had almost kissed her, and she'd almost let him.

She'd seen the pictures of him with countless women in the papers, she knew he had dozens of females chasing him, and she didn't intend to fall prey to his charms or money and become another notch on his bedpost.

She couldn't allow a kiss to happen. She stiffened her spine, stared out at the passing brush, at a loon in the distance, then vaulted from the truck when he stopped in front of the cottage.

"Thanks for the tour," she said. "I'll review the horses' medical files and get started this afternoon."

"Sure."

She hurried inside, retrieved Johnny's photo, and walked to the cafeteria for lunch. The rustic building was filled with long wooden tables, a salad bar, hot dishes, cold plates and sandwiches, an ice cream and dessert island and a drink stand with jugs of homemade sweet tea, lemonade and bottled water and sodas. Already a dozen men, dusty from working with the cattle and horses, had filed in and were heaping their plates with the entrée of the day—meat loaf made from Flint's own prized beef cattle.

Preferring her heavier meal at night, she opted for a turkey sandwich and fresh fruit, then carried her plate and a bottle of water to one of the tables. It was easy to see the division of laborers: the cattle hands tended to stick together, as did the grooms and horse trainers.

She imagined Johnny would have sought a job as a groom, so she joined that table but was well aware that some of the men at other tables were eyeing her openly. She offered them a friendly smile, but an elderly Hispanic man frowned at her, so she turned away, then introduced herself to the employees at her table.

"I'm Dr. Lora Leigh Whittaker," she said. "I'll be working with the horses, so if you detect any problems, please let me know."

A young brunette named Kiki grinned and introduced herself; then the four men at the table followed suit. They chatted for several minutes, exchanging general information about their backgrounds and experience.

"I heard someone mention that I should talk to a groom named Johnny. Do any of you know where he is?" Lora Leigh asked.

Kiki frowned. "We don't have a groom named Johnny. Maybe you've got the name wrong."

Lora Leigh shrugged innocently. "Probably so. This is my first day. I've met so many people, I'm confusing names."

She desperately wanted to show them her brother's picture, but if she aroused suspicion, one of them might report her to Flint. Maybe she'd find that list of employees in his files. He might even have photos of them attached to their applications.

She finished up, then excused herself and walked to the vet clinic, grateful that Carol had left for lunch and the office was empty. She settled at the main computer and began to search through the files for Flint's employee list. Medical records on the horses were easily accessible, and she made a mental note to review them to verify that Flint treated his animals with the care he professed.

Yet when she tried to tap into the employees' files, she came to an impasse—she needed a password.

She tried variations on the ranch's name, Diamond Daddy, Flint's name, then his birthday, which she'd found in one of the many articles on him.

She drummed her fingers on the desk in frustration. Nothing worked.

She'd have to sneak into his home office and see if she could find an employee list and his password there.

The sooner she found out what had happened to Johnny, the sooner she could leave the Diamondback and Flint McKade behind and move on with her life.

FLINT STRODE INTO HIS office, irritated with himself for his lack of control with Lora Leigh. It was her first day, for God's sake, and he'd tried to get up close and personal.

While she might have disliked him before, her opinion of him had probably taken a drastic downhill slide, any respect he might have earned from his ranch operations evaporating.

Lucinda had left a stack of pink message slips on his desk, and he thumbed through them, noting that several were from charity event planners, one was from Akeem, telling him that a memorial service had been planned for Viktor in two days, and a third was from Amal Jabar, his Middle Eastern contact who'd arranged for the Arabians to be imported. According to Amal's message, he'd questioned his men but hadn't learned anything suspicious.

Flint picked up the phone to return Amal's call, but a knock sounded at the door, and he glanced up and saw Detective Brody Green poke his head in. "McKade?"

He nodded. "Come on in, detective."

The sandy-haired cop loped in, his mouth set in a stern line, his eyes perusing the room and taking in the Triple Crown trophy. "Impressive. I watched the races and couldn't believe how fast Diamond Daddy was."

"He is a great Thoroughbred." Flint gestured toward the leather chairs facing his desk. "Would you like coffee or a cold drink?"

Detective Green shook his head. "No, thanks. Just finished lunch."

Flint nodded and sat down, planting his hands on the desk. "What did you find out about the attack last night?"

The detective removed a pocket-size notepad and

glanced at it. "Nothing concrete yet. The medical examiner verified your pilot's ID, as well as that of the older man, Grover Harper, but there's a problem with the younger man's identity. You said you didn't know him?"

"I have a lot of employees in different capacities, Detective. I don't know them all personally."

"You don't interview them?"

"My manager Jose Ortega is in charge of hiring the ranch hands and Reba Bales oversees the horse people, trainers, assistants and grooms. Didn't he have ID with him?"

Detective Green made a clicking sound with his teeth. "That's just it. He did. Name on the ID is Huey Houston, but in the DMV records, we found two Huey Houstons. One is eighty-five years old and in a nursing home in Corpus Christi, and the other died five years ago in a car crash in Austin."

Flint frowned. "I don't understand. You're saying this guy used a fake name?"

The detective shrugged. "Looks that way. If he were Hispanic, I'd think he was an illegal, but this guy was Caucasian. Could be he'd had trouble with the law and wanted to hide out on your land."

Flint squared his shoulders. "If he was a criminal, you think he might have had something to do with the sabotage?"

"It's a possibility. We're running DNA, checking prints and looking at dental records, but that will take time." Detective Green leaned forward, with his elbows on his knees. "Meanwhile, I'll need a list of all your employees."

Flint's pulse pounded. "You think this was an inside job?"

"Whoever did this had knowledge of your plans, the time your shipment would arrive, where the plane would land."

Flint shifted, anger mounting in his gut. He didn't like suspecting his own people.

"Who all was involved in this shipment?" Detective Green asked.

Flint rapped his fingers on the desk. "My business manager, Simon Cornwall, of course. Reuben Simms, the pilot who brought them in. Amal Jabar. He's my Middle Eastern contact who helped arrange the importation. Then the two hands who were on board." He paused, seeing their bloody faces in his mind.

"Who else?" Detective Green asked.

Flint sighed. "My partners in the Aggie Four, and Deke Norton of Norton International. But they all had vested interests in the Arabians."

Detective Green pursed his mouth. "I'll still need to talk to them. Any problems between you guys?"

"No," Flint said. "Not at all. I'd trust any one of them with my life."

Detective Green gestured toward the computer. "Now that list?"

"Right." He clicked a few keys, entered his password, then accessed the file and hit Print. While they waited, Detective Green pressed on.

"Can you think of anyone with a grudge against you?"

Flint scowled, then rubbed the back of his neck. He didn't want to point the finger at anyone without conclusive evidence.

"Come on, McKade," Detective Green said. "A man in your position and with your wealth has to have made enemies."

Flint hesitated, then nodded. "I admit that some people don't like me, but I don't think any of them would commit murder."

"They could have been after the shipment. Then something went wrong, and they had to shoot their way out," Detective Green suggested. He gestured toward the legal pad on Flint's desk. "Make a list."

The printer had finished, so Flint handed the employee list to the detective, then glanced at his legal pad. Once he jotted down names, Detective Green would question everyone on the list. If they disliked him now, they would hate him after the police treated them like suspects.

But the bloody scene on the plane flashed in his head, and he knew he had to explore any possibility. Those men deserved justice.

"Tate Nettleton," he said as he scribbled his half brother's name.

"Who is he?"

"My half brother, or so he claims. He showed up a while back, long after my father died, and declared that he was his son. I asked him to have DNA tests to prove it," Flint said grimly. "Meanwhile, I gave him a job. A few weeks later, I caught him trying to steal my cattle, so I fired him and told him never to come back."

"I assume he didn't take your dismissal very well."

A muscle ticked in Flint's jaw as he recalled the ugly scene. "He threatened to get back at me."

Detective Green made a clicking sound with his teeth. "All right. Who else?"

Flint sighed and scribbled another name. "Lawrence McElroy. He owns Stone Creek, east of here. He was pissed when I bought Diamond Daddy out from under him at auction."

Detective Green raised a thick brow. "And Diamond Daddy won the Triple Crown last year."

"Yeah. We just retired him to stud."

"You'll make a mint from stud fees, right?"

Flint nodded.

"Sounds like motive to me," Detective Green muttered. "Anyone else?"

Flint chewed the inside of his cheek, then jotted down another name. "Howard Reed. He was going into fore-closure in December, so I bought him out. I paid a fair price for his land, but he accused me of cheating him and filed a lawsuit."

"It's still pending?"

Flint nodded.

"Is that it?"

For a brief second, Flint thought about Lora Leigh's iciness but dismissed it. She wouldn't do anything to jeopardize the horses.

"That's all I can think of for now."

"One last thing," Detective Green said. "I'll need copies of your financial statements for the last two years and your insurance information."

Flint froze, a seed of suspicion sprouting. "What for?"

The detective's mouth tilted into a lopsided grin. "Just to verify that you didn't sabotage your own shipment for the money."

Flint gripped the desk edge. "You need a subpoena for that."

Detective Green stood, squaring his shoulders. "I can do that. But if you want to be eliminated as a suspect, then you'll cooperate."

"Trust me, I don't need money and would never endanger an animal for insurance purposes." Cold rage swept through Flint, but dammit, if he didn't cooperate, he'd look guilty.

"Then fax me the records," Detective Green said as he rose and lumbered toward the door.

"Fine," Flint said between clenched teeth.

Detective Green left, and Flint grabbed his hat and left for the funerals. On the ride to town, he phoned his sister Taylor, who handled his accounting, and asked her to fax the information to Detective Green.

During the next two hours of back-to-back funerals, he said goodbye to his men, vowing silently as he stood by their graves and consoled their families that he would find their killer.

No sooner had he started for home than Flint's cell phone rang. It was his cattle foreman. "Yeah, Flint here."

"Hey. We've got some fencing down near Little Bluff. We're trying to herd the cattle back inside and get the fence repaired, but I thought you'd want to know."

"I'll be right there."

"And, Flint…"

"What?"

"It looks like the fencing was intentionally cut."

Chapter Five

Lora Leigh decided to familiarize herself with the animals in her care, so she reviewed the charts for each of the Arabians and the quarter horses, noting their diet supplements, the results of blood tests, documents for the state and federal government-required testing, as well as the results of tests conducted to make sure the mares were healthy enough for impregnation.

So far, the records indicated Flint took exceptional care of his horses. There was nothing there to impugn his character.

She spent the rest of the afternoon tending to various tasks. She treated one of the quarter horses for an ankle injury, took blood tests to determine if two of the mares were pregnant, then conducted wellness checks on each of the stallions.

Finally, as the sun began to set and dusk settled over the property, she rode back out to check on the Arabians. The barn was virtually empty as the grooms had left for dinner, and she slipped inside. Sir Huon edged up to the stall door to greet her, leaning his nose through the stall bars for her to pet him. She laughed and moved from one horse to the next, taking her time to talk to each animal, admiring their coats, stance and spirited nature.

Eastern Promise seemed sulky and shook her head at Lora Leigh as she approached, backing away. Lora Leigh studied the magnificent creature, a seed of worry sprouting inside her.

All their paperwork and preliminary tests looked good, and their vaccinations were up to date, but she'd do blood work of her own to confirm they were healthy. She retrieved her medical kit, took the blood samples and labeled them to send to the lab. Then she palpated each horse, taking more time with Eastern Promise, who seemed to grow irritable at her touch.

She soothed her with gentle words and strokes, but her eyes appeared glassy, raising Lora Leigh's anxiety level. Should she tell Flint she suspected the horse might be ill?

No. It was too early to tell.

Eastern Promise was adjusting to her new environment. Some horses were more sensitive and needed longer to adjust to new situations and stables than others.

"It'll be all right, girl," she murmured. "I'll take care of you. I promise."

The sound of footsteps shuffling across the dirt floor jarred her, and she turned, expecting to see one of the grooms, but the silhouette of a lanky man wearing a white Stetson, a checked shirt and jeans appeared behind her, his face shadowed by the wide brim of his hat. He smelled like sweat, cigarette smoke and stale beer; if he worked for Flint, he was obviously drinking on the job.

Which immediately put her senses on alert.

He swaggered toward her, planting one arm on the wall beside her, pinning her in, and she noticed a jagged scar along his chin. His eyes were gray, cool, chilling. "Well, hey there, sugar. Where'd you come from?"

She squared her shoulders and faced him, trying a direct approach. "I'm Dr. Whittaker," she said bluntly. "One of the veterinarians on staff. And you are?"

"Name's Tate. I'm Flint's brother."

"Really?" She arched a brow. "I didn't realize he had a brother."

His mouth thinned into a straight line. "Well, that's 'cause I'm not one of the rich, spoiled McKades. But I should have been."

She frowned in confusion, yet the animosity in his tone sent a frisson of alarm up her spine. She stepped sideways, nearing the wall to put some distance between them. Behind her, Iron Legs kicked at the stall door, and the other horses whinnied, as if they sensed tension in their midst.

"Do you work here?" Lora Leigh asked, trying to calm the horses by maintaining a level tone.

He made a dismissive sound. "No, I was looking for Flint. Someone told me they thought he'd be out here with his new prized animals. Hell, I figured he'd sleep in the barn with them."

His bitter tone told her it was best not to antagonize him. "I'm sorry. He was here earlier. Maybe you should try the main house."

"Hmm." He leaned closer, then braced one hand against the wall, pinning her in again. "I think I like it better here. Scenery's nicer."

Lora Leigh gritted her teeth, forcing herself to keep her cool. If she pushed this guy's buttons, things could get ugly real fast. "The horses are lovely," she said, ignoring his lecherous look. "But I'd better get going. I still have rounds to do. And I'm supposed to meet Flint to give him a report on the Arabians."

A bald-faced lie, but she didn't care. Instincts warned her to stay on guard and to get away from this guy.

She pasted on a saccharine smile, then ducked below his arm and reached for her medical kit and the vials of blood she'd collected for the lab.

But Tate grabbed her wrist and she jerked her head up. "Excuse me?" she said.

"Take your hands off of her, Tate."

Tate froze, his fingers tightening around her wrist. Lora Leigh glanced up and saw Flint a few feet away, his massive outline shadowed by the last strains of sunlight fighting through the darkening sky. Tate looked dangerous, but Flint looked downright menacing, a force to be reckoned with as he stalked toward his brother and dared him not to obey his command.

RAGE BOILED INSIDE Flint. It was bad enough that Tate had tried to steal from him, but manhandling one of his female employees was intolerable.

He should have filed charges against Tate before. If he discovered Tate was behind the attack at the airport, the broken fencing he'd spent hours repairing, or if Tate touched Lora Leigh again, he would make sure his sorry ass rotted in jail.

The fact that Tate was here now and that there had

been trouble on the ranch today seemed downright suspicious.

He contemplated the best way to handle the bastard. The only thing that would appease Tate was money. Maybe he should offer him a lump sum of cash to leave town. It might be the only way to get rid of him for good.

But he couldn't do that, not if he'd killed his men.

"Tate," he said in a lethally low tone, "I said let her go."

A chuckle rumbled from Tate as he released her and threw up his hands, feigning innocence. "Hey, brother, no harm. Just talking to the help."

Lora Leigh's lips thinned, from his brother's remark or the situation, Flint wasn't sure which.

"Are you all right?" he asked.

She shot him an irritated look, as if to say she could have handled Tate without his interference, but she didn't know the scum like he did.

"I'm fine. I just told your brother that I had to meet you to discuss the Arabians."

Flint met her gaze and nodded. "That's right. Now, what did you want, Tate?"

Tate loped toward him, and Flint detected the scent of beer. Not a good sign. Tate was a mean drunk. Couple that with his bad attitude, and he could be dangerous.

"Heard you got in some new beauties," Tate said, then glanced at Lora Leigh. "I came to see the Arabians, but hell, I got more than I bargained for. Seems like you've brought in some other lookers around here."

Flint hooked his thumbs in his belt loops in a relaxed

stance, but every bone and muscle in his body was primed for battle. "You've been drinking, Tate. You shouldn't have driven out here."

Tate tipped up the brim of his hat. "Just a couple of beers. Don't you make the lady here think you're some damn saint." He turned to Lora Leigh, belligerence in his cocky look. "Don't let him fool you, Doc. He takes care of himself and nobody else."

"Look, Tate," Flint snarled. "I don't have time for your crap. My best friend just died, three of my men were killed in an attack last night, and I've been repairing fences cut by a vandal this afternoon. I told you to stay away from here, and I meant it."

Much to his relief, Lora Leigh didn't react. She swept past him, with a tilt of her chin. "I have some blood work to get to the lab. I'll talk to you later, Flint."

He nodded, gripping his hands into fists as she strode to the door and walked outside, her demeanor professional, as if she hadn't been rattled by Tate's crude behavior. But he'd seen the hint of fear in her eyes when he'd walked in, had heard the slight waver in her voice.

If Tate had noticed it, he hadn't reacted. But he didn't doubt that his smarmy half brother would take advantage of her slight size and the fact that she was a woman, if for no other reason than to piss him off.

"Did you cut my fences?" Flint asked bluntly.

Tate's gray eyes flared, although he swayed slightly, indicating he'd had more than a couple of beers. "In spite of what you think, I have other things to do than spend my days concentrating on destroying you."

"So you do want to destroy me?"

Tate shifted, his angular face blanching. "That's not what I said."

"Then what are you doing here?"

Tate rubbed his face, and Flint zeroed in on the scar on his chin, the one he'd no doubt earned in a barroom brawl. "I told you, I came to see the Arabians. I do have an interest in horses and the ranching business. If you'd only given me a shot."

"I did," Flint said through a growl. "But you tried to steal cattle. I should have had you arrested, so consider yourself lucky." He jerked the collar of Tate's checked shirt. "But that was a onetime deal. Mess with me, any of my animals or my employees again, and I'll see that you pay."

He hauled Tate outside and shoved him toward his truck, then glanced in the truck bed. Wire cutters.

Rage darkened Flint's face as he removed them from the truck and examined them. "You cut my fence, didn't you?"

"No," Tate said, with a steely look. "But you're making me wish I had. Now give me back my cutters."

"No way," Flint growled. "Get the hell off of my land, and don't come back."

Tate muttered a string of obscenities, then jumped in his truck and barreled down the dirt drive, sending dust and gravel flying.

Flint watched him leave with trepidation. He should have sucked up his pride and paid off the jerk. But he couldn't stomach rewarding someone for being a lazy, mean SOB.

He wiped at the perspiration trickling down the back of his neck. He had a bad feeling that he hadn't seen the last of Tate. That if Tate hadn't caused his current problems, he would do something to retaliate against him now. No man liked to be bested in front of a woman.

Especially a man like Tate Nettleton.

LORA LEIGH TRIED TO SHAKE off the uneasy feeling Tate had given her as she carried the blood samples into the vet clinic, but Flint's reaction to the man had cemented her first impression that he could be dangerous.

She also didn't want to feel bad for Flint, but he'd sounded truly grief stricken when he'd mentioned the loss of his best friend. She'd seen the news article about Prince Viktor Romanov's death in the paper. Photos of Flint with the prince had filled the society pages over the past months, and the business sections of newspapers had highlighted the charitable efforts of the Aggie Four Foundation, created by Flint, the prince, Akeem Abdul and Jackson Champion.

Carol was shutting down her computer as Lora Leigh entered the clinic, and smiled up at her. "How was your first day, Dr. Whittaker?"

"Fine. And please call me Lora Leigh." She gestured toward the blood samples she'd drawn from the Arabians. "Can you please send these to the lab ASAP?"

"Certainly. The courier usually stops by twice a day. He should be here any minute."

Lora Leigh stored the vials in the refrigerator and filled out the necessary lab order, detailing the tests she wanted run. Carol had grabbed her purse and was on her way out the door when the courier arrived and collected the samples.

Once they left, Lora Leigh reviewed the past two years' worth of medical files, noting details regarding the horses' feeding regimens, injuries and illnesses, and their exercise and training schedules, but again, every file indicated the most humane treatment of the animals and their excellent health care.

The door squeaked open, and she jerked her head up, afraid Tate had found her again, but Flint's broad body filled the doorway. She quickly clicked to shut down the computer.

His wide mouth was set in a grim line, but he removed his Stetson and scrubbed his shaggy hair back from his face. Even dusty and sweaty, with his brown eyes hooded with anger, he looked impossibly sexy.

"I came to apologize for Tate," he said in a thick, dark voice. "He has a beef with me, but he has no right to intimidate the people I work with."

"Don't worry about it," Lora Leigh said, with as much conviction as she could muster. "I can handle myself."

Some emotion flickered in his eyes, and he harrumphed. "Maybe, but he's a mean drunk and untrustworthy. He's been warned to stay off the property, so if you see him or he bothers you again, please let me know." He hesitated, then added, "And I am sorry about earlier."

She nodded, then pushed away from the desk and stood, moved by the sincerity in his voice. Had Tate cut the fence, or could Johnny possibly still be around? And if he was, why wouldn't he let her know?

Flint's masculine scent drifted toward her, his concerned look an indicator that the prince's death, the attack on his shipment, the murder of his employees, weighed heavily on him.

For a brief moment, her heart went out to him, and she itched to assure him that everything would be all right.

But her brother's face flashed in her head, and she bit back a comment. She had to keep their relationship on a business level until she found Johnny.

And if he'd hurt her brother, she would go to the police.

"How did everything else go today?" he asked. "Any problems?"

She hesitated. "The broodmares look good," she said. "I also took some blood work from the Arabians."

"I didn't realize it was time for more tests."

"Actually, Eastern Promise seemed a little sulky and irritable, so I wanted to run my own tests."

The worry in his eyes deepened, faint lines from the sun creasing around his eyes. "You think she's sick?"

"I don't know," Lora Leigh said. "It's possible she's just traumatized from the move. But I tend to err on the side of caution."

He nodded. "I trust your judgment."

Guilt assaulted her. He shouldn't trust her, not when she wanted to ruin him.

His cell phone rang, and he checked the number. "Sorry. It's my sister. She does accounting for me. I need to get this."

"Of course." She set about organizing the charts for the interns.

A few minutes later, Flint disconnected the call, with a weary sigh.

"Is something wrong?" Lora Leigh asked.

"She said someone tried to hack into my employee records this afternoon. Coupled with everything else that's going on, it does appear that one of my employees has a grudge against me."

She tensed, wondering if they'd figure out that she'd been trying to hack into the files.

Then he shocked her by reaching out and gently touching her arm. "Watch your back, Lora Leigh. If you see anything suspicious, don't try to deal with it. Call me immediately. Okay?"

Once again, guilt slammed into her. He sounded so sincere, so…protective.

But if he knew the real reason she was here, he would fire her on the spot.

Which meant she had to find that password and see if her brother's name was on the employee list, if there was any record of him. Or if he'd just disappeared, and it was time for her to call the police and report him missing.

Anxious to get away from Flint, she headed outside to her Jeep. She hurried to the cafeteria and ate, noting that the dinner turnout was much lighter than the breakfast or lunch turnout. Most of the employees probably had dinner with their families.

Something she would be doing if her father hadn't killed himself and Johnny hadn't set in motion his plan for revenge.

Once she finished, she decided to drive back out to the barn and check on the Arabians before she went to bed. Although the interns took night duty, worry knotted her stomach. She wanted to see Eastern Promise for herself.

Night had set in, the moon only a sliver of light above the barn, storm clouds obliterating the stars. She glanced around to make sure Tate hadn't returned, but there were no vehicles in sight, so she climbed out and walked toward the barn. The horses neighed and whinnied, and she slipped inside the barn, speaking softly to soothe their distress. But just as she approached Eastern Promise's stall, the barn lights flicked off.

She spun around, the hair on the back of her neck prickling. "Who's there?"

Remembering Flint's warning, she scrambled to find a pitchfork or something else to defend herself, but footsteps sounded. Then, suddenly, something sharp slammed against the back of her head.

A piercing pain shot through her skull, and she collapsed, the world spinning as she lapsed into darkness.

Chapter Six

As Flint headed up the staircase, toward his suite to shower before dinner, Lucinda called him from the foyer. "Flint, it's Roy Parkman. He says there's trouble and needs to talk to you."

Holy hell. What now?

He rushed down the steps two at a time and yanked up the phone. "It's Flint. What's wrong?"

"I'm out at the barn with the Arabians," Roy said, sounding out of breath. "I found Dr. Whittaker on the floor, unconscious."

He clenched his jaw. "Is she all right?"

"She's rousing, but she might have a concussion."

Flint kept a doctor on staff at the ranch for the employees. "Call Dr. Hardin. I'll be right there." He grabbed his Stetson and his keys and jogged outside to his truck, then flew the mile and a half to the barn. What had happened? Had one of the horses kicked her? Had she fallen?

Or had there been foul play?

Roy's Explorer was parked next to Lora Leigh's Jeep

when he arrived, and he threw his truck in park. In light of his recent problems, he scanned the premises in case Lora Leigh had been attacked and her assailant was hanging around, but found nothing amiss, so he went inside the barn.

His chest tightened when he spotted Lora Leigh lying on the concrete floor near the back stall, Roy kneeling beside her. The horses were whinnying, stomping, and pacing, obviously agitated and spooked, so he checked their stalls to make sure no one was hiding inside.

"Shh, guys. Everything's all right," he murmured, then hurried to Lora Leigh, stooped down beside her and gently examined her head. A small spot of blood matted her hair and a lump was forming, but Roy had pressed a cloth to it and placed one of the clean horse blankets under her head for a pillow.

Rage bolted through him as she moaned and tried to open her eyes.

"Did you see anyone?" he asked Roy.

The craggy-faced ranch hand shook his head. "No, but the barn was dark when I drove by. I thought that was odd, what with Dr. Whittaker's Jeep parked outside."

Flint ground his teeth. "Calm the horses and check them over. I'll wait here with Lora Leigh for Dr. Hardin."

Roy nodded and went to do as he was asked. Flint stroked Lora Leigh's cheek, forcing a calm into his voice when anxiety riddled him. "Lora Leigh, it's me, Flint. Can you hear me?"

Her eyes slowly opened; then she blinked several times, as if to focus, and frowned. "What happened?" she whispered.

"I was hoping you could tell me," he said, his voice cracking slightly. "One of my hands found you here, unconscious, on the barn floor. Did you fall?"

She lifted her hand to her wound, then tried to sit up, but he gently urged her to stay still. "Just rest. The doctor will be here any minute."

"I don't need a doctor," she said stubbornly. "It's just a bump. I've had worse from riding falls."

"Listen, Lora Leigh, I'm not taking any chances," Flint said. "Now lie back and tell me what happened.'

She exhaled slowly, as if the movement cost her. "I came to check on the Arabians one more time, but then the lights flicked off, and someone hit me from behind."

The door squeaked open, and Jesse Hardin shouted his arrival.

"Back here," Flint yelled.

Seconds later, the fifty-something doctor examined Lora Leigh and confirmed that she had a bruise and a cut but didn't need stitches. "You'll probably have a whopper of a headache tonight, and you'll need to be watched."

"That's not necessary," Lora Leigh protested.

"I've got it covered," Flint said, cutting her off. "She'll stay in the main house so I can watch her."

Lora Leigh glared at him and once again struggled to sit up, but she swayed and he caught her, supporting her against his body. "Don't be stubborn, Lora Leigh. You're a doctor. You know the drill for a possible concussion."

She flashed him another defiant look, as if the thought of staying in the same house with him was appalling.

He didn't give a damn. Someone had nearly killed

her on his property. Someone who was trying to sabotage him, it appeared, in any way they could.

He removed his cell phone from the clip on his belt to call Detective Green. To hell with pissing off his employees. He was going to find out who was doing this and put an end to it now, before anyone else got hurt.

He had three deaths on his conscience. He didn't want Lora Leigh's name to be added to the list.

LORA LEIGH WANTED TO SCREAM that she wouldn't stay in Flint's house, that she didn't want his care or concern—or the guilt she heard in his voice—but it was obvious that he wasn't going to listen to her.

The stubborn, bossy man.

He angled his head and looked at her as he asked the detective to send out a crime-scene unit, his eyes so smoky and almost...possessive...that something fluttered low in her belly, and she amended her thoughts.

The stubborn, bossy, sexy man.

The idea that someone was compelled to take care of her was foreign to her. Her father had been protective but had aged before he died, and without her mother, she'd taken care of him and Johnny.

She rubbed her scalp, struggling to recall the details of the attack. Who had assaulted her? She didn't have any enemies.

Was it possible that someone on the ranch had discovered that she was related to Johnny, that she'd come here to snoop around, and wanted to keep her from finding out the truth?

The doctor cleaned her wound and applied antiseptic, then patted her arm. "Call me if you need anything, you hear? Flint McKade is a good man, and he'll take care of you tonight."

She nodded. So far, everyone she'd encountered on the ranch had spoken highly of Flint.

Flint shifted his stance. "I'm going to meet Detective Green here and have him search the premises for forensic evidence. Did you touch your attacker, Lora Leigh? Maybe fight back?"

She struggled to remember again, but the past hour was a blur, so she shook her head. "No, he came at me from behind. I didn't get a chance to fight back."

"So it was a man?" asked Flint.

She frowned, then nodded. "He smelled like cigarettes and sweat."

Flint glanced around the barn, as if searching for the weapon that had struck her head. "All right. But we should bag your clothes for the police. Maybe they'll find a hair or some trace evidence to nail this guy."

The doctor helped her to stand. "You may want to check on her a couple of times in the night," he told Flint.

"Don't worry," Flint said. "I will."

She started to argue that she was fine alone, but Flint's black look cut her off.

"I'll drive her to the house," Dr. Hardin offered.

She leaned against the doctor. "Just let me stop by the cottage and pick up a bag."

"I'll meet you there after the detective arrives." Flint walked her out to the doctor's car and helped her get in it. "And please rest, Lora Leigh. You'll have all the time off you need to recover."

She met his gaze, the tender concern in his gruff voice almost bringing a tear to her eyes.

He must have mistaken her reaction for fear, because he placed his hand over hers and squeezed it. "Don't worry. I'll find this guy. If he tries to hurt you again, he'll have to come through me. I promise."

She nodded, but once again, guilt weighed on her. Had she misjudged Flint so horribly?

Or was he simply concerned about liability for his employees, and the possibility of lawsuits and his reputation being tarnished, because of the recent murders?

FLINT MET DETECTIVE GREEN at the barn door and showed him in, then explained where they'd found Lora Leigh. "I glanced around for a weapon but didn't find one," he said.

Detective Green frowned and tugged at the waistband of his pants. "I'll check around. Did she get a look at her attacker?"

"No. He hit her from behind. And unfortunately, she didn't get a chance to fight him."

"Maybe he left a print or a button or something."

Flint scratched his chin. "I can't figure out what in the hell he was doing in here. There's no sign that the attacker had a trailer outside, which would indicate he'd come to steal the horses. And if that was his plan, why not wait until the middle of the night, when everybody was asleep?"

Green made a clicking sound with his teeth. "Good point. Maybe he was going to harm the horses."

Flint's blood turned to ice. "That's damn cold."

"Yeah, but whoever is doing this is playing hard."

Flint conceded that it was a possibility, then watched as Detective Green dusted for prints along the stall rails and walls.

"There are several prints," Detective Green said, with a scowl. "I'll need to compare them with those of your employees."

Flint accepted the intrusions, hoping it wasn't one of his men conniving behind his back.

Detective Green stooped and raked aside some straw with his fingers, then lifted a small scrap of flannel material, which had caught on a loose nail. "I'll bag this as well."

The detective searched for another half hour, then the two of them locked up and Flint walked him to his police cruiser. "I think you need to call all your employees together," Detective Green said. "Let's have a sit-down and see if anyone acts suspiciously."

"You're going to be there?" Flint asked.

Detective Green dropped the evidence bag into a box on the backseat of the cruiser. "Yes. I want to question each and every one of them."

Anxiety clawed at Flint, but he agreed, although he dreaded the meeting.

Weary, he drove back to the main house. Thankfully, Lucinda had showed Lora Leigh to the upstairs suite across from his. He knocked on the suite door, but when she didn't respond, he grew worried and eased open the door. Lora Leigh stepped from the bathroom in a satiny robe that clung to her curves and made his body go instantly hard. Her hair was damp and cascaded around her shoulders in wavy curls.

Instantly, her chin went up, and she tugged the robe up to her neck.

He didn't know if her resistance over staying in his house was due to her independence or her determination to keep her distance from him, but he refused to let her stay alone until this culprit was caught.

"I just wanted to check on you," he said. "How are you feeling?"

She pressed a hand to the back of her head. "I'm fine. I told you, it's just a bump."

He ground his teeth. "If you need anything, just call. I'm right across the hall."

She frowned and glanced at her computer on the desk in the corner. "Thanks, but I'm sure I'll be all right."

"Did you have dinner yet?" Flint asked.

She nodded. "I ate at the cafeteria earlier."

He hesitated, his hand on the doorknob. "If you want something else later, a snack or drink, just let Lucinda know. Or you can make yourself at home in the kitchen."

"Thanks. But I'll probably just go to bed."

His pulse pounded. He was reluctant to leave her. "I'm really sorry about the attack, Lora Leigh. I've never had trouble like this before."

An odd expression flashed in her eyes. "I'm really okay, Flint. Don't worry."

Easy for her to say. She didn't have three men's deaths on her conscience. "If you want to take a leave until we find who's sabotaging me," he said in a gruff voice, "I'll understand."

She stared at him for a long moment, then shook her

head. "No, I'm here to do a job, and I intend to do it. No one is going to run me off."

He remembered the sight of her lying on the barn floor and how his heart had hammered in his chest, and he started to reach out, intending to push the damp hair from her cheek.

But he held himself in check. She'd made it clear she wanted to keep their relationship on a professional level, and he had to respect her wishes.

But he didn't like it one bit. Because Lora Leigh was smart and strong and tough.

A woman he could like.

A woman he was definitely attracted to.

If she'd only give him a chance.

Then again, he didn't need a personal entanglement right now. If someone wanted to hurt him, they might come after anyone he cared about.

He didn't want her death on his head, too.

HOLY MOTHER OF GOD. HE couldn't believe that vet had returned to the barn. What poor timing. He hadn't had an opportunity to finish the job.

And with the cops crawling all over the place, it would make it even harder. What if he'd left a print or some other piece of evidence behind?

What if Flint had figured out who he was and what he was doing?

And if Dr. Whittaker continued to get in the way, next time she wouldn't get off with just a knot on the back of her head.

He'd have to kill her.

A smile curved his lips. If it came down to that, he could make it look as if Flint had done it. Ahh, that would be sweet.

Then the rich bastard would rot in jail and be out of the way forever.

Chapter Seven

Flint checked his messages and found one regarding Howard Reed's lawsuit against him, so he phoned his lawyer. "Hey, Bill. It's Flint."

"Howdy, McKade. I thought I'd update you on the case."

Flint massaged the back of his neck, wishing for once he'd get some good news. "Yeah?"

"I've tried to settle, but Reed is still ranting about being wronged. It looks as if you may have to take the case to court."

Flint didn't have time to deal with this crap. He hadn't wronged the man; he'd just bought his land when he went into foreclosure. "Look, up the offer and tell him that's the final one. If he doesn't settle, I'll play hardball, and everyone in Texas will know just how in debt he was, and the reason for it." According to Flint's sources, the lowlife had cheated on his wife with several underage prostitutes and had paid sorely to keep them quiet.

"It's time you played dirty and showed him what you're made of," Bill agreed. "I'll make the call ASAP."

Flint hung up, cursing the fact that people wanted to blame everyone but themselves for their problems.

Finally, he went upstairs to bed, but sleep eluded him. He tapped on Lora Leigh's door and heard noises from the other side, so he slipped inside to check on her.

The covers were tangled around her bare legs as she tossed and turned, small moans vibrating from her lips.

He eased himself down on the side of the bed and stroked her hair. "Shh, Lora Leigh. It's all right now. You're safe."

She made a soft crying sound, and he pulled her into his arms. "It's all right. I'm here now."

She curled against him, her body quivering as he gently stroked her shoulders and back. "Flint…"

He traced a finger along her jaw. "You were having a bad dream."

A rosy blush crept up her face. The faint moonlight spilled into the room, highlighting her golden hair and delicate features. God, she felt like satin and softness and made his body rock hard and achy.

"I'm sorry," she whispered.

He thumbed a silky strand of hair from her eyes. "No, *I'm* sorry. You wouldn't have been hurt if you weren't working for me."

She bit down on her lip, her breath fanning his neck as she looked up into his eyes. "I'm okay now," she said softly. "I didn't mean to disturb your night."

He smiled, itching to lower his mouth and taste her. She disturbed him on a lot of levels, yet he sensed her comment had been an invitation for him to leave, so he traced her cheek with the pad of his thumb, then climbed from her bed and walked to the door. But when he reached the hallway, he turned back.

"Remember, if you need me, I'm across the hall."

He waited a second, half hoping she'd ask him to stay, but when she didn't, he went into his room and shut the door. A cold shower later, he tried to sleep, but images of dead bodies and sick horses and Lora Leigh's pale face as she lay on the barn floor after the attack haunted him.

He paced his room for a while, then checked on her again, the night stretching with worry.

"Flint, please, stop hovering," Lora Leigh said when she entered the kitchen for coffee the next morning. "I'm perfectly fine now. My head doesn't even hurt."

He gave her a dark look. "I'm sorry. Having my employees attacked on my ranch doesn't sit well with me. I'm protective of my own."

An odd look flickered in her eyes, and she glanced into her coffee, her mouth pursed. His cell phone rang, and he glanced at the number.

His sister, Taylor.

"Sorry, but I need to answer this."

"Of course." She went into the dining room for the breakfast Lucinda had laid out and he connected the call.

"Hey, Taylor. What's up?"

"I heard about the upcoming funeral for Viktor. I'm so sorry, Flint. I know how close you two were."

Grief crowded his throat. "I still can't believe he's gone. I keep expecting him to call me and stop by like old times."

"I hope they find out who killed the royal family," she said worriedly. "And, Flint, have the police found the person behind the trouble with the Arabian shipment?"

"Not yet. Now, how are you, sweetheart?"

Taylor sighed. "I'm hanging in there," she said quietly. "I worry about Christopher, though. He needs a male role model."

"I'm here for him and for you. I love you, Tay."

"I love you, too. I was hoping we could come and stay at the ranch for a few days."

"You know I'd welcome that," he said, "but last night one of my vets was attacked, so I think it'd be better if you stayed away. I don't want to take a chance on endangering either one of you."

"All right. But keep me posted, Flint." Her voice sounded strained, almost teary. "And please be careful. I don't want to lose you."

"Don't worry. That's not going to happen."

He hung up, rubbing at his chin. He was worried about his little sister, but he didn't want her or her son anywhere near his ranch. They were the only family he had.

The thought of Tate's visit the day before rose to taunt him. Tate wasn't family, and he'd never think of him that way.

Tate had been pissed at Flint for firing him. And he'd been flirting with Lora Leigh.

He hadn't returned last night to attack her, had he?

LORA LEIGH SMILED AT LUCINDA as she searched online recipes on the computer in the kitchen, then stepped into the dining room and chose fresh fruit and muffins from the breakfast array, cocking her ear to hear Flint's conversation. But all she heard was him calling someone sweetheart and saying that he loved her.

An odd feeling tightened her chest, although she didn't understand the reason. The papers portrayed Flint as a ladies' man and eligible bachelor, but she hadn't realized he had a serious girlfriend or lover. But his tone indicated he cared about this woman, as he didn't want her around the ranch in danger.

She should be glad to know that he was taken. All the more reason to avoid getting personal and not to feel guilty over using him.

When he entered the room, their gazes locked, and something smoky lurked in the depths of his eyes. He was so big and tough looking, so rugged, yet last night he'd held her so tenderly that butterflies had fluttered in her stomach.

Why did Flint make her body warm? Make her wish that things were different? Make her feel safe and protected…and needy in ways she hadn't felt in a long time?

"Are you all right, Lora Leigh?" he murmured. "Your cheeks look flushed."

Heat flooded her, and she sipped her coffee in an effort to curtail any more sexual thoughts. "It's just the heat," she said, willing her body not to respond to the sultry sound of his voice. The night before, when she'd curled against his hard body and sunk into his arms, she'd wanted him to stay, to hold her all night. To touch her in secret places.

And she'd wanted to touch him all over.

But touching him was too dangerous.

"Really?" He stepped closer, so close she smelled the faint scent of soap on his bronzed skin, the scent of his masculine body, and felt the heat radiating off him. "Are you sure that's the problem? Maybe you need to go back to bed."

She gritted her teeth as an image of him in bed with her flickered through her mind. "What I need is to work. How about you? Plans today with your girlfriend?"

He frowned as she gestured toward the phone. Then a sly smile slid onto his face, and he leaned forward, with a teasing grin. "That was my sister, Lora Leigh. I don't have a girlfriend." He lowered his voice. "In fact, there's no one special in my life at all."

She gulped back her embarrassment, wishing she'd kept her thoughts to herself. Now, heaven help her, his eyes sparkled with hunger and she saw the seductive allure that made half the women in Texas swoon.

Irritated, she quickly reminded herself she was immune to his charms. "Well, it's really none of my business. I just didn't want you to think that you needed to babysit me."

A deep chuckle rumbled from his chest. "I wouldn't call it babysitting," he said, then sobered. "But I will protect you as long as you work for me."

Which wouldn't be for long.

She couldn't let him mess with her mind. It didn't matter if he hated her when he found out why she'd come here.

She had to discover the truth about her brother.

"Detective Green asked me to call my employees together. He wants to talk to them," he informed her as he headed to the door. "We're meeting in the cafeteria at seven, before everyone gets busy for the day." He hesitated. "He'll probably want to talk to you about last night."

Lora Leigh twisted her clammy hands together. "I'll be there."

In fact, having all the employees together would make it easier for her to search for Johnny. Maybe he was still on the ranch, safe and sound and in hiding.

She only hoped that Johnny hadn't done something illegal, and that he wasn't responsible for killing Flint's men.

FLINT SHOWED DETECTIVE Green into his home office and offered him coffee, then asked Lora Leigh to join them. He introduced them.

"How do you feel this morning, Dr. Whittaker?" Detective Green asked.

Lora Leigh feigned a smile. "I'm fine, thank you."

Detective Green sipped his coffee. "Can you tell me exactly what happened last night?"

She swallowed back a sudden case of nerves, then explained that she'd been worried about the horses and had stopped by the barn to check on them. "Then I heard footsteps and turned, but someone struck me on the back of the head." She paused. "I wish I could be of more help, but I never saw him."

Detective Green studied her for a moment. "All right. I'll let you know if forensics turns up anything."

Lora Leigh stood. "Thanks. Then I guess I'll get to work."

"Remember to meet us at the conference room of the

cafeteria," Flint said. "It'll give me an opportunity to introduce you to my staff."

"I'll be there," she replied.

Flint watched her leave, wishing she'd take the day off, but the woman was too damn stubborn.

Detective Green cleared his throat. "I spoke with Lawrence McElroy. He has an alibi for the night of the airport attack and for last night."

Flint scowled. "McElroy would have hired someone to do his dirty work."

Detective Green nodded. "I'm aware of that. He's still on our suspect list."

"Who else did you talk with?"

"Your partners at the Aggie Four and Deke Norton," Detective Green grunted. "They all speak highly of you and seemed concerned about your welfare."

"They're good friends," Flint said. "You're wrong to think for a minute one of them would betray me."

"Maybe," Detective Green conceded, although his expression remained wary. "I also checked out Reuben Simms, your pilot. Did you know he was heavily in debt? That he had a gambling problem?"

Flint frowned. "No, I didn't know."

Detective Green arched a brow. "Maybe he was in on it and got killed in the cross fire. The same goes for the two ranch hands."

"Grover would never do anything illegal," Flint said sternly. "The man didn't give a hoot about money."

"I've tried to get in touch with your Middle Eastern contact, but he hasn't returned my calls," Detective Green said.

Flint shrugged. "Jabar is hard to reach sometimes, but I got a message from him assuring me that none of his people were involved."

"Maybe he's left the country for good." Detective Green tapped his notepad. "I've been thinking. If the motive wasn't to steal the horses, perhaps he was running some kind of smuggling operation."

Flint sipped his coffee, lost in thought. "I don't think so. I've worked with him for years. He is a friend of Akeem's, and I've never had any problems. I've also overseen personally every shipment that's come through and never noticed anything suspicious." He drummed his fingers on the desk. "Yesterday someone cut down my fencing in the northwest pasture, and then the attack occurred last night in the barn. Both of them sound more like someone wanting to cause me trouble, not a smuggling ring. Did you check out Howard Reed?"

Detective Green nodded. "He's not your friend, that's for sure. But he insists that he's taken the legal route with the lawsuit, so why would he risk losing by sabotaging you or commiting murder?"

Flint hesitated. "I guess that makes sense."

Detective Green checked his watch. "It's time to meet the rest of your crew."

Flint grabbed his Stetson and gestured toward the door. Five minutes later he studied his employees as they gathered in the large conference room of the cafeteria. His managers, office assistant, vets, ranch hands, grooms, trainers and assistants were all there. He couldn't believe that one of them would betray him or murder his people to hurt him.

But it was possible, and he had to let Detective Green question them.

Of course, in doing so, he'd piss some of them off, and he might even lose a few workers.

But he had to find out who'd killed his men before the SOB took any more lives.

AS FLINT INTRODUCED LORA Leigh to his workers, she scanned the sea of faces, searching for her brother in the crowd, but didn't spot him anywhere. Disappointment and anxiety ballooned in her chest.

Where are you, Johnny? And what have you gotten yourself into?

"I'm sorry to have to call everyone together," Flint said. "But I know you've all heard about the attack on the Arabian shipment and the deaths of three of my men."

Whispers echoed through the room as various men shot nervous glances at one another.

Flint cleared his throat. "And last night, Dr. Whittaker was assaulted in one of the barns."

More nervous rustling, then Flint gestured toward Detective Green and introduced him. "You've all heard my creed, my basic rules. Hard work, loyalty, honesty and respect… We take care of our own." He paused. "So if one of you knows something, please share it with Detective Green."

A Hispanic man in his forties waved a hand, and Flint addressed him. "Yes, Ortega."

"Does this mean you think one of us sabotaged the shipment and attacked the doctor?"

Jake Kenner, the new trainer that Flint had introduced to Lora Leigh, caught her eye with a worried look. Reba Bales shifted and rubbed her arms, and several of the ranch hands grumbled protests. Roy Parkman, the man who'd found Lora Leigh in the barn the night before, loped in and took a seat, but he looked pale and covered a cough with a handkerchief.

"Everyone stay calm," Flint said. "It's just routine. Detective Green is questioning all my friends, coworkers and employees, so please don't take offense. Also, I need everyone to be on the lookout for anything suspicious. If you see a stranger lurking around or anything that seems out of place, contact me immediately."

Detective Green began to divide up the group for questioning, and Lora Leigh excused herself to check on the horses.

First, she drove to the quarter-horse stable, where she saddled a chestnut named Sly. She rode him to the stables housing the broodmares. There she made routine rounds and examined two pregnant mares. Then she stopped by the vet clinic to check for messages and address any problems noted by the night shift. Carol was at the meeting, so she checked the files and found the fax of the lab results on the blood work she'd done on the Arabians.

Worry knotted Lora Leigh's stomach as she studied the lab's findings. Eastern Promise's white cell count was low; so was Iron Legs'. It could indicate an infection, even equine flu. Grabbing her medical bag, she hurried outside, then rode over to the barn housing the Arabians.

With the employees at the meeting with Flint, the barn was empty, except for the horses. "Hey, buddy," she whispered as she approached the first stall.

Sir Huon and Lord Myers both neighed and whinnied, bobbing their noses for attention, and she moved from one to the other, scratching behind their ears. "You guys are so beautiful. Getting used to your new home?"

Sir Huon rubbed his head against her, and she laughed and hugged his neck, speaking softly to him, then moved on to check the others.

Iron Legs was eating, but Eastern Promise seemed lethargic.

"Hey, girl." She moved into the stall, speaking softly, trying to soothe the animal. Already she noted signs that she was sick: a clear nasal discharge and a cough.

She took her temperature and found it high, then discovered her submental lymph nodes were swollen.

Not a good sign.

This shouldn't be happening, not with the vaccinations in order.

So why was Eastern Promise ill?

With equine influenza, symptoms could worsen rapidly. Thankfully, her limbs didn't appear swollen, but if she developed pneumonia, it could be dangerous.

She had to begin treatment, start antibiotics and isolate her.

But Eastern Promise had been with the other Arabians for days now. What if it was too late and they became ill, too? All the Arabians could be infected.

She had to alert Flint. But with all his other problems, she almost hated to bother him.

Then another disturbing thought struck her. The Arabian shipment had been attacked, and someone had been in the barn last night and assaulted her.

Was there a connection?

Could someone have intentionally given the horses something to make them ill?

She'd have to conduct more tests to determine exactly what they were dealing with, if this really was the flu or something that mimicked its symptoms.

Something that could prove deadly and indicate sabotage.

Chapter Eight

Flint checked the roster of employees with his managers and discovered two men missing: Pedro Gonzalez and Emanuel Sanchez.

"What's the story?" he asked Ortega. "Are they illegal? Green is going to want to know."

Ortega hunched his bony shoulders and averted his gaze. "*Sí.*"

"*Sí,* what? They're illegal?"

"They have paperwork," Ortega said in a thick accent. "And they're good men. Just want to earn a living for their families."

Flint frowned and read between the lines. "But you're not sure their paperwork is legit." He pulled Ortega aside and lowered his voice. "I told you I don't mind helping your friends or family, but it's important to me to run an aboveboard business. That's why I offer benefits and housing. But I have to follow the law, and so do you."

"I'll see if I can find them," Ortega said, with an apologetic look.

Flint studied the man. Ortega had worked for him for several years now, and he trusted him. But his family had suffered, and he wanted to give back to those trying to cross the border and find work. "You have twenty-four hours to bring them to me, or I'll report them to Green."

Flint's cell phone rang, and he checked the number, then tensed when he saw it was Lora Leigh. Had she been attacked again?

Surely not in the light of day.

He gave Ortega another stern warning, then left the room, where Detective Green was still questioning his men, and connected the call. "Hey, it's Flint."

"Flint, it's Lora Leigh. I'm out here with the Arabians." Her voice sounded strange, worried. "What's wrong?"

"Eastern Promise is exhibiting symptoms of equine flu, but I need to run more tests to verify what we're dealing with."

He scrubbed his hand through his hair. What else could go wrong?

"I'm sorry, Flint," she said softly. "The preliminary blood work I did yesterday shows a low white cell count. I want to start antibiotics and move on to more extensive testing. If this is equine flu, we need to stop it from spreading."

Hell, yes, they did. He didn't want any animal to suffer or die. Not on his watch. "I'll be right there."

He quickly stepped inside, told Detective Green where he'd be, then saw Roy Parkman coughing and burying his head in his hands. Frowning, he strode over to the man.

"Roy, you okay?"

The older man looked up at him with glazed eyes,

and Flint reached out and touched his forehead. He was burning up. "You're sick, Roy. Go see Dr. Hardin now."

"I have to work," Roy insisted. "Those Arabians—"

"Are in good care with Dr. Whittaker," Flint said, although a frisson of alarm ripped through him. Eastern Promise was sick with flu-like symptoms. Now Roy.

What in God's name was going on?

Flint stooped and patted the craggy-faced man on the back. Roy had been a dedicated employee for ten years. "You have sick days, Roy. And I need you healthy." He purposely gentled his voice. "So please go see the doc and get some rest. And if you need medication or anything else, your insurance covers it."

Flint glanced up at Jake Kenner. "Jake, do you mind escorting Roy to the doctor?"

"Sure thing." Jake took Roy by the arm, steadying him when he wobbled sideways. "Come on, old man. You need to go to bed for a while."

Roy told him not to call him old but followed Jake outside.

Flint was on their heels and drove to the barn to check on Lora Leigh and the Arabians. Doubt, anger and fear twisted in his gut.

Last night Lora Leigh had been attacked in the barn housing his new imported horses. Had her attacker done something to Eastern Promise to make her ill?

He'd never had a shipment attacked until he decided to branch out into this breed.

Did the attacks have something to do with the Arabians, or were they just an attempt to destroy him? Who hated him that much?

FLINT LOOKED SO UPSET as he rushed into the barn that Lora Leigh almost went to comfort him.

But he was the enemy.

Only the sight of his big masculine body as he knelt to examine Eastern Promise and the tender way he soothed the animal made her momentarily forget that he was the reason her father had committed suicide. That he might know what had happened to Johnny…

What if her brother had stumbled upon the person trying to sabotage Flint and had been hurt in the process?

Or what if he was the culprit?

She tried to banish the thought as Flint turned dark, concerned eyes toward her. "She has a fever?"

Lora Leigh patted the horse's neck and nodded. "Her eyes are weak. She has a mucous discharge from her nostrils and swollen lymph nodes."

Eastern Promise had sprawled on her side, her head drooping sideways. "You're going to be okay, baby," he murmured. "You're in good hands, I promise."

He motioned Lora Leigh outside the stall. "How can she have equine flu if she was vaccinated? Were all the vaccines in order?"

"Yes," Lora Leigh said. "At least according to the paperwork. Occasionally, an animal is resistant to the vaccine, though, or…"

"Or what?"

"Or we could be dealing with a new strain of influenza or another disease entirely, one that mimics the symptoms of equine flu."

Flint's massive shoulders stretched the crisp denim shirt, reminding her once again of his utter masculinity.

If she didn't detest him so much, she'd feel compassion for him now.

She certainly did for the horses.

"How do we proceed?"

Lora Leigh folded her arms. "I'll conduct a battery of tests and consult with a specialist at the research center at A&M."

Flint sighed, a sound full of anxiety. "You sensed something was wrong the first time you saw them, didn't you?"

She bit her lip. "Well, actually I thought Eastern Promise seemed sulky and moody, but sometimes it takes animals a few days to adjust to new surroundings."

"I appreciate your insight," Flint said. "And the fact that you didn't go running after last night."

Once again, guilt pricked her, but she squared her shoulders. "I'm not afraid of confrontation, Flint. Or of a challenge."

A small smile curved his mouth, a pleasure in light of his brooding manner when he'd entered the barn. "I'm not afraid of a challenge, either. And I'm not going to let whoever sabotaged me, killed my men and hurt you escape without being punished."

His protective tone warmed her insides and sent her pulse soaring.

But what if Johnny was part of the problem? Could she stand by if Flint hurt him, or if he put her brother in jail?

Worry lines creased his eyes. "We have to separate Eastern Promise, don't we?"

She nodded. "She'll need at least six weeks of

complete rest. The ventilation is key as well, and so is treatment. I'll start the tests on her and the others right away. Also, dispose of any water and food supplies. They might be contaminated."

Her comment brought a frown to his face. "Lora Leigh, I have to ask you a question. A while ago, I noticed Roy coughing, and he's running a fever. Is it possible that he caught an illness from Eastern Promise?"

Lora Leigh's stomach plummeted. "It's hard to say without testing."

"But is it possible?"

She hesitated, inhaled a deep breath, then nodded. "Ask the doctor to run his blood work, and limit the number of people who come in contact with him. Also, anyone who comes into contact with the Arabians should take precautions. I'll call my contact at the research center now. Let's act fast so your entire horse population isn't endangered."

As THE DAY AND EVENING dragged on, worry and anger gnawed at Flint. If someone had intentionally hurt his horses, he wanted them in jail.

He'd never had problems with equine flu and didn't like the prospect of word traveling and tarnishing his reputation. Just the mere thought of an influenza epidemic or possibly West Nile virus would send investors, potential clients and breeders running for the hills.

Flint admired Lora Leigh's insight and professional manner as she took charge. She gently soothed Eastern Promise as she separated her from the other Arabians, then called the specialist and administered more tests to all the horses in the barn.

That night she coordinated around-the-clock supervision for the Arabians, making certain each of the interns was gloved and masked.

The next afternoon, Flint checked his watch. It was time to leave for Viktor's funeral. Before he left for town, though, he rode out to check on the Arabians and Lora Leigh.

"Eastern Promise is about the same, but she's resting," Lora Leigh said. "But Sir Huon is acting sulky now, so I'm concerned about him."

Flint removed his Stetson and scraped his hair back from his forehead. Lora Leigh looked exhausted but beautiful, even garbed in a mask and gloves. But her eyes warned him that the animals were still in danger.

"Any results from the tests?" Flint asked.

She shook her head. "No. I'll let you know as soon as we hear."

He reached out and squeezed her arm. "Thank you, Lora Leigh. I feel so much better knowing you're here."

An odd look flickered in her eyes, and she averted her gaze. "I'll do whatever I can to save them and make sure they're healthy."

He gave her a grim look. "I'm on my way into Kingsville for Viktor's funeral. I'll be back later, but call me if there's any change."

"Of course. How's Roy?" Lora Leigh asked.

"I talked to the doc this morning. He's worried about a lung infection, and unfortunately, Roy's not responding to the antibiotic."

"Did he hospitalize him?" Lora Leigh asked.

Flint gritted his teeth. "Yes. He's developed pneumonia."

"Oh, Flint, I'm so sorry."

Her soft voice twisted his insides. She sounded so sincere, caring. And she obviously loved the horses and ranch life as much as he did.

Unlike most of the women he'd met since he'd accumulated his millions—women with ulterior motives, women who wanted to use him to climb the social ladder. Women who wanted his money and connections.

Lora Leigh was different. She was a giver, not a taker. A woman without her own agenda.

She sighed and rubbed her arms, and he read fatigue in her body language. She had a head injury but was working diligently to save his animals.

He was beginning to really like her.

And he wanted to hold her, tell her how much he admired her work, her professionalism, her…everything. That she was someone he could care about.

But Eastern Promise snickered, and she turned back to the horse, so he said nothing. Now wasn't the time.

He had to meet the other Aggie Fours and inform them about his latest problems.

Grief welled in his chest. First he had to face the funeral today, so he rushed home and showered, then dressed in his black jeans and duster and drove to Kingsville. Outside the church, friends had gathered to commiserate, and others moved quietly inside the chapel. He parked and spotted Akeem, Jackson and Deke Norton waiting together on the manicured lawn. Shoving his hands into his pockets, he walked toward them, the mood somber.

A month ago the Aggie Four had gathered to toast the deal for the Arabians, the optimistic future of Viktor's country, Rasnovia, and the good that the Aggie Four had helped to accomplish for its citizens.

Today, there was nothing to celebrate: the country of Rasnovia was in turmoil, as were Flint's own business and future.

But today was devoted to mourning his friend.

He joined Akeem and Jackson, and they shook hands and all agreed to speak to the crowd in Viktor's honor. Then they would say goodbye to him forever.

And the Aggie Four would become three.

LORA LEIGH TRIED TO HOLD on to her disdain for Flint, but she couldn't help but sympathize with him and his problems. She hated to see any person or animal suffer.

Exhausted and grateful that the intern had come to take his shift watching Eastern Promise, she rode Sly, the chestnut quarter horse, back to the stable, unsaddled him and brushed him down, then drove to the main house for a shower, a meal and some sleep.

Flint hadn't returned from the funeral yet, and Lucinda was in the kitchen, supervising the meal, so she decided this might be her only chance to slip into Flint's office and search for his password.

Flint's basic rules taunted her. Everything he'd professed to value matched her own values, making guilt prick at her for sneaking behind his back.

Troubled by her physical attraction to the man and

the fact that she was starting to soften toward him, she slipped into his office. Lucinda had mentioned that he'd probably have dinner with his friends after the funeral service. She glanced at her watch and rushed to his desk, then began to dig around inside.

She'd find his password, then access his files and see if Johnny was listed as an employee. Once she learned her brother's alias, she'd question Flint's ranch family and find out exactly what had happened to him.

FLINT STARED OUT AT THE crowd, his throat thick with emotions. "Viktor Romanov was an inspiration to his family, his friends and his countrymen. He leaves behind a legacy for the Rasnovians to fight for, for his friends to maintain, for his followers to live up to."

Tears burned his eyes as grief consumed him, but he blinked furiously to stem them. The sight of the Aggie-filled church resurrected fond memories of his youthful days on campus, of the first moments of his friendship with Viktor, as they'd bonded over talk of lost fathers, of fledgling dreams, of girls and romance and their goals to overcome any obstacles thrown in their path to success. For them, failure had never been an option.

Neither had dying young and being alone.

He cleared his throat. "We will all miss Viktor. Let us honor him today and the legacy in the work he did for his people. If we can follow his example, we'll make our world a better place."

Fearing his sorrow was going to overcome him, he stepped down from the podium and pinched the bridge of his nose.

Technically, each of the Aggie Four had achieved financial success beyond their college dreams, yet sometimes Flint still felt as if something was missing in his life.

His family, for one.

Granted, he had Taylor and his nephew. But no lover who truly cared for him.

Sure, a lot of women had romanced him. Seduced him. Offered him companionship and a warm bed.

But their affection and attention had come with a price.

A price he hadn't been willing to pay.

He wanted the real thing. The kind of love his parents had had, even when money had been scarce, food short and quarters cramped.

Lora Leigh's face flashed into his mind, and he glanced at his friends as he reclaimed his seat. What would they think of Lora Leigh?

Would they understand his attraction to her?

Could he possibly have found someone special in his life? And could he win her trust and affection?

He certainly had to try. He didn't want to die like Viktor, an accomplished man, but one without a significant other. He wanted a woman to love, a family, a son or daughter to carry on the legacy he'd built.

The priest finished the eulogy; then the crowd began to disperse, and his friends stood.

"You want to grab a steak?" Jackson said.

Flint hesitated. Normally, he wouldn't turn down dinner and beer with the Aggie Four. But tonight he felt an urgency to return to the ranch.

"I think I'll take a rain check," he said. "I need to check on things at the Diamondback." He explained about the attack on Lora Leigh, the Arabians and the possibility of an equine flu outbreak, his belief that someone was out to destroy him.

"Let us know whatever we can do to help," Akeem said.

Jackson grasped Flint's hand. "We'll help you find out who's doing this, Flint. If they hurt you, they hurt all of us."

"Thanks," Flint murmured, always amazed to have found such a brotherhood. "I appreciate your support."

"I'll talk to Sylvester Robbins and explain that there will be a delay in moving some of your stock to the auction house," Jackson said. "But I'll keep a low profile on the exact problem."

Deke Norton looked somber. "I definitely want to find out who has endangered the Arabians. I planned to invest in them, and someone is threatening that investment."

"I'll keep you posted," Flint said. He glanced again at the dispersing crowd, thinking he should mingle and get reacquainted with some of his college friends. But the Diamondback came first. And the weight of Viktor's absence made it difficult to talk, much less be sociable. All he wanted was a stiff drink, to forget his problems for a minute and mourn his friend in peace.

And to see Lora Leigh.

He said goodbye, then hurried to his truck and drove back to the Diamondback, his anxiety mounting as he approached the ranch. Normally, a sense of peace washed over him at the sight of the engraved wooden sign at the entrance, the lush greenness of the land and his prized horses galloping in the pastures. But today tension knotted his shoulders, and the air was stifling, as if he could detect the scent of danger nearby.

He threw a mental lasso around his imagination, reminding himself that Lora Leigh would have phoned if the horses weren't all right. And if there'd been another fence break or attack on one of his hands, someone would have called.

As he parked and let himself inside the house, he chalked his nerves up to Lora Leigh. He'd never had a woman tie him in knots when he hadn't even kissed her, much less slept with her.

But the more time he spent with Lora Leigh, the more attracted he was to her. The more he wanted to be with her. And not just in her bed.

The house seemed quiet as he entered, the smell of roast beef and potatoes wafting in the air. But a faint light glowed in his office, which sent a frisson of alarm up his spine. His managers knew his office was off-limits except when he was present.

Maybe the person sabotaging him had sneaked inside.

Trying to keep his boots from clattering on the polished marble floor, he crept toward the heavy wooden door, then inched up to the edge and peered inside.

His pulse pounded at what he saw.

Lora Leigh was in his office.

And not just inside, but in front of his computer, rummaging through his desk, as if she was searching for something.

What in the hell was she looking for?

He gripped the door handle as he ticked off the events of the past few days in his head. Lora Leigh arriving the night of the airport sabotage. Her cool reaction to him when they met.

Taylor's phone call warning that someone had tried to hack into his files.

Cold anger and a sense of betrayal raged through him, and he muttered a curse. He'd trusted her. Hadn't suspected that she had a secret agenda. Had hired her because he'd sympathized with her and the loss of her father.

Was she behind the sabotage at his place?

Chapter Nine

Lora Leigh jerked her head up, her stomach plummeting when she spotted Flint in the doorway of his office. A cold mask slid onto his face, hardening his features and making him look intimidating as he strode toward her.

"What are you doing, Lora Leigh?"

She bit her lip, her mind racing for a possible explanation. "I needed to look at some files."

He arched a dark brow, and before she could close the computer files, he moved around the desk and encircled her wrist with his fingers. Their gazes locked, the heat radiating off him so intense that she swayed slightly. His scent invaded her, potent and masculine, but anger and suspicion darkened his eyes.

"What files?"

Her heart thundered in her chest. "Flint, I can explain."

He glanced down at the screen, his eyes narrowing as he realized that she'd accessed his employee files. She had finally found his password, had hacked into the files and had been scanning each one for her brother. As she'd hoped, Flint had photos of each employee on file, along with background checks, notes on the interviews and the employees' experience as well as letters of reference. She'd combed through the grooms and hadn't found Johnny, so she had decided to search the ranch hands for the cattle operation.

Confusion registered on his face, but he didn't release her arm. "Why did you need to look at my employee records? Were you looking for the person who attacked you?"

He'd given her a way out. She should take it. But she was tired of sneaking around. With the dangerous circumstances surrounding the Arabians and time ticking away, she needed answers.

She just prayed Johnny was alive and not in trouble, or else she'd be betraying him and he'd never forgive her.

"Lora Leigh," he said in a lethally calm but demanding voice. "You said you could explain."

She closed her eyes, vying for courage. At first she'd suspected Flint might have done something to Johnny, but after the past couple of days, she couldn't imagine him hurting, much less killing, someone.

Suddenly he released her arm. "Tell me what's going on. What are you doing in here?"

The slight hint of hope and trust in his voice, the fact that he wanted her to explain, compounded her guilt.

"Tell me, Lora Leigh. Why are you going through my files?"

Hurt flickered across his face, making her feel so small, she wanted to disappear into the woodwork.

She swallowed her nerves and decided to come clean. If he hadn't hurt Johnny, maybe he'd help her find him.

That is, if he didn't throw her off the Diamondback tonight. "I was looking for my brother."

A long, tense second passed. He was studying her, trying to decide if she'd lied. "Why would you think you'd find something about him in my files?"

God help her, she hoped she wasn't making a mistake in trusting him. "Because he came here a few weeks ago and took a job."

Flint tipped back the brim of his Stetson and scratched his head. "I don't recall hiring anyone else named Whittaker."

A drop of perspiration trickled down the back of her neck as she sank into the chair, exhausted. "He might have used an assumed name."

His eyebrows shot up, but he hesitated before replying, obviously trying to piece together what she was telling him. "I don't understand. Why use another name? Has he been in trouble before?"

She sighed, leaned her elbows on the desk and propped forehead in her hands. "No, well, he's been drinking ever since Daddy died. But he doesn't have a record, if that's what you mean. He just didn't want you to know who he was."

A heartbeat passed; then his boots clicked on the wood floor as he paced the room. When she finally summoned enough courage to look at him, he was standing at the window, staring out, a somber expression on his chiseled face. When he turned to look at her, the disappointment in his eyes sent a pang to her chest.

"He blames me for your father's death, doesn't he."

It wasn't a question, but a cold, hard statement.

She nodded, her throat thick with worry. Guilt. Regret. Fear.

"Do you?" he asked quietly.

The sense of betrayal reverberating in the two words made her heart ache. "I…did."

He exhaled and scrubbed his hand over the coarse stubble on his jaw. "And that's why you accepted the job here? Not because of all the bull you gave me about admiring my operation?"

"I did it to find Johnny," she said earnestly. "He called me and told me he landed a job here, at the Diamondback. I made him promise not to do anything rash and to keep in touch." Her voice wavered. "But I hadn't heard from him in over two weeks, and I was worried."

His gaze met hers, and a vein pulsed in his neck. "And what did your brother think he'd accomplish by working incognito here?"

She had to look away, couldn't stand the condemnation in his eyes. "I don't know."

"Yes, you do, Lora Leigh." His voice turned harsh. "He wanted to find something to impugn my character or to ruin me. That's why he took an assumed name."

Her pulse pounded. "Maybe."

He fisted his hands by his sides and jammed his face close to hers. The scent of his raw anger nearly knocked her over. "How far would he go to get revenge on me?"

She knotted her hands in her lap, striving to remain calm, but everything was spiraling out of control. "I'm not sure," she whispered through a dry throat. "Like I said, he took Daddy's death hard, was lost, was drinking way too much…"

"Do you think he's responsible for the attack at the airport? For my men's deaths? For the Arabians getting sick?"

"No," she whispered, although her protest sounded weak to her own ears.

"You do, don't you? You think he might be involved." He slammed his fist on the desk. "Would he hurt you, too, to get revenge on me, Lora Leigh?"

Tears blurred her eyes. "I honestly don't know," she murmured. "Johnny had been out of control. Losing the ranch was the last straw. I tried to talk some sense into him, but he wouldn't listen."

Still, she should have tried harder to stop him from coming here. He was her little brother, the only family she had left.

If he was in trouble or dead, she'd never forgive herself.

Just as she couldn't forgive herself for her father's suicide. If she hadn't sucked so much money from the family for college, if her father hadn't taken a second mortgage out to pay for her vet school, he might not have lost the ranch.

Then he'd still be alive. And she and her father and Johnny would be home, working the Double W, where they belonged.

A SENSE OF BETRAYAL AND disappointment filled Flint as he studied Lora Leigh. For God's sake, he had been in mourning for Viktor and had imagined coming back to the ranch and finding Lora Leigh in his home, then sharing dinner and conversation with her and maybe…a kiss.

And more.

How could he have been such a fool?

"I'm sorry, Flint," Lora Leigh said softly. "But he's all the family I have left. I can't lose him, too."

He clenched his jaw. He didn't want to have any compassion for her, but he sensed she was genuinely worried about her brother and frightened for him, too.

"If you came here looking for your brother," he said in a measured tone, "why didn't you just ask me, Lora Leigh? Why the hidden agenda?"

She sighed shakily, twisting her hands together, and rose from the desk to face him. Remorse and guilt glistened in her eyes, and the truth dawned on him, with sickening clarity.

"Because you thought I might have found out what he was up to and done something to him," he said gruffly.

She clamped her teeth over her lower lip, and anger churned in his gut.

"That's it, isn't it? What did you think I'd done, Lora Leigh?" She averted her gaze, but he gripped her arms and forced her to look at him.

"You thought I'd hurt him, didn't you?" His voice rose in disbelief and rage. "Don't tell me you thought I was capable of murder?"

She shivered beneath his hands. "I…didn't know," she said in a strained whisper.

He sucked in a sharp, painful breath, pushed her away from him and strode across the room, needing distance and time to calm down. "Dammit, Lora Leigh, you must really think I'm a bastard. You must hate me."

She walked over to him and touched his back, but he jerked away.

"Flint, I...don't know what to say. I'm sorry...I was just so worried about Johnny. I didn't know what else to do or who to trust...."

He steeled himself, his chest aching. Women had used him before, had wanted his money, a piece of his land, his prestige, but no one had ever thought he was a coldhearted killer.

The fact that Lora Leigh didn't trust him cut like a knife, twisting through his heart.

Hardening himself as he reined in his temper, he fisted his hands by his sides, then glanced at the computer. "Did you find him?"

She shook her head and wrapped her arms around her waist.

"Did you go through all the photos?"

"No." She reached inside the pocket of her jeans and pulled out a worn photograph, then held it out to him. "But this is what he looks like. He's only twenty-two, just a kid, really."

His hand was amazingly steady as he took the photograph. The brush of her fingers over his triggered a frisson of sexual awareness.

And another pang in his chest.

He'd thought he might have something special with Lora Leigh, but any thread of hope had been severed like a frayed rope.

He had to focus on business. He'd find her brother and then deal with her. His employees were like family to him; he'd told her that.

Hell, she must have been laughing behind his back. Perspiration beaded on his brow as he studied the photograph of the young man. Blond hair, blue eyes, early twenties, he looked youthful as he stood between Lora Leigh and her father.

"Do you recognize him?" Lora Leigh whispered.

He shook his head. "No. But you know how many men I have working for me. I don't interview them all."

And Johnny might have avoided meeting him.

"I'll fax copies to my managers and see if they recognize him." He moved to the desk with rigid shoulders, sat down, scanned the photograph, then set up the fax, along with a note of instructions. "I'll also have them show it around." He met Lora Leigh's wary gaze. "If he's on the ranch, we'll find him."

"Thank you, Flint." She tucked a strand of her ponytail behind her ear. "I...don't know what to say, except that I'll understand if you want to fire me."

He did want to fire her for lying to him, for her ulterior motives. In fact, he wanted her off the ranch as soon as possible so he wouldn't have to look at her beautiful face and want her.

Because, dammit, in spite of what she'd done, he had the insane urge to drag her into his arms and hold her. To bury himself in her silky hair and lush body and erase the agony in her eyes.

And the hurt that she'd caused him by distrusting him.

He wanted to convince her he wasn't that ruthless man.

That he was honorable and decent, and that he understood her grief, because he was grieving for a lost loved one, too.

But he restrained himself. Couldn't allow himself to want her or feel anything for her. Not again.

He'd help her locate her brother, then make them both leave the Diamondback.

"Flint?"

"No," he said, remembering the sick Arabians. "I need a vet for the horses, and you're the most qualified person I know."

A wary look flickered in her eyes. "I'll stay and take care of them until you find a replacement."

He gave a clipped nod. His cell phone rang, and he glanced at the number. Jake Kenner. Lora Leigh's pager went off, and they both tensed.

"It's the clinic," she said.

He quickly connected the call to Jake.

"Flint, Lady Luck is foaling, but she's in trouble," Jake said. "I'm trying to reach Dr. Whittaker."

"She's here with me. We'll be right there."

He disconnected and glanced at Lora Leigh, heading to the door as he explained. It was going to be a long night.

But he remembered that Lora Leigh had been attacked and knew that as difficult as it was to be around her, he had to stay with her for her protection.

But as she retrieved her medical kit and they climbed in his truck and drove to the stable, a disturbing thought struck him. The police and the medical examiner still hadn't identified the young man who'd been murdered on the plane. He'd had fake ID on him.

What if he was Lora Leigh's brother? What if he'd been killed because he was working for Flint?

Jesus.

Then Lora Leigh would have even more reason to hate him.

HE PACED THE BARN, WIPING at the sweat dripping down his face, his cell phone plastered to his ear. "I told you I've been looking, but I haven't located the merchandise."

"You have to find it immediately. If McKade discovers it and turns it over to the cops, our entire operation could go sour."

He cursed. "Don't you think I know it? My ass is on the line here, too."

"So is mine. Now do the damn job I hired you to do, or you'll be sorry."

His heart raced as more sweat slid down his brow. "You wouldn't do that. I can ID you."

"Not if you're dead," he growled. "Don't forget, if you decide to run your mouth, I know where your family is."

The phone went silent, and he threw it across the barn, sputtering a litany of curses. He wished he'd never gotten involved in this scheme. Wished he'd turned down the money.

But his family, his little girl, had desperately needed it for medical care. She would have died without the kidney transplant.

It was too late to go back now. He had to keep silent and do as ordered, or it would all have been for nothing.

Chapter Ten

Lora Leigh would never forget the hurt look on Flint's face when he realized her subterfuge.

They rode in silence to the stable, the tension thick, his anger palpable. Maybe she should have confronted him in the beginning about Johnny, but she'd been too afraid of Flint...and she'd feared that Johnny had done something illegal.

And it was possible that he had.

Flint would hate her if Johnny was responsible for the trouble on his ranch. And if he'd killed those men...

No, her little brother wouldn't resort to murder.

So where was he now?

Jake waved to them as they entered the stable, and she saw the mare lying in the birthing stall. Her breathing was erratic, and she moaned and kicked, obviously distressed.

"How long has she been in labor?" Lora Leigh asked.

Jake shrugged. "About twenty minutes."

A sliver of unease rippled through Lora Leigh. Labor usually went swiftly for mares.

"There, there, Lady Luck. It's going to be okay." She knelt and patted the horse's head gently, stroking her and speaking low to calm her.

Flint knelt to check the mare as well, his gaze meeting hers. "She's going to be all right, isn't she?"

She nodded. "I think so, but let me examine her."

She donned gloves and palpated the horse to check the position of the foal. "She's almost ready."

The next hour was strained and exhausting as she and Flint worked in tandem to keep the mare calm, comfortable and to help her deliver the foal. Lady Luck panted, weakened from the ordeal, and Lora Leigh soothed her again with a gentle pat.

"Come on, Lady Luck. You can do it," she whispered. "Just hang in there."

A minute later, the foal finally slid out, and a sense of elation washed over her.

Flint breathed a sigh of relief and smiled, but his smile died when he met her gaze.

Guilt assaulted her, along with regret. She could no longer deny that she admired Flint, that he had earned his reputation and cared for his animals and employees.

But he'd still bought out her father's ranch. And her father would be alive if he hadn't.

Lora Leigh dipped the foal's navel in antiseptic to prevent infection; then Lady Luck licked the foal clean. She laughed as the foal tried to stand, wobbling on unsteady thin legs, and the mare lifted her head up to watch.

Lady Luck had passed the placenta, and Lora Leigh examined it to confirm that no fragments had been left behind in the mare, as that could cause her to develop an inflammatory condition.

"You did good, Lady Luck," Lora Leigh murmured. The foal began to nurse, and Lora Leigh smiled, a sense of joy filling her.

Satisfied that mother and baby were going to be all right, she cleaned up, not surprised that Flint helped. He not only ran the operation here, but he actually worked the ranch.

Jake, who had gone to check on the other animals, reappeared. "How is she?"

"Everything's fine," Lora Leigh said. "But I'm going to stay with her for a while."

Flint frowned. "Is there something you're not telling me?"

Lora Leigh nodded. "No. I just want her to be watched."

"Then I'll call the intern," Flint said curtly. "That's their job."

Lora Leigh glanced down at the mother and baby. "I really don't mind." Besides, she'd feel more comfortable sleeping in the stable than she would in Flint's house. Especially after their earlier confrontation.

"I said the intern would stay," Flint said sharply.

Flint's cell phone trilled, and he frowned, then connected the call. "Dr. Hardin, what's wrong?"

She tensed, her pulse hammering as Flint's face twisted in distress. "Thanks for letting me know, Doc."

When he hung up, he scrubbed a hand over his face, his jaw set tightly.

Unable to resist, she reached out and pressed her hand over his arm. "What's wrong, Flint?"

"Roy Parkman died a few minutes ago. They're going to do an autopsy."

Lora Leigh shuddered. What if he had had the same flu strain as the Arabians? Then not only were the Arabians in serious danger, but so was everyone who'd been in contact with the horses.

FLINT SILENTLY SWORE AS he and Lora Leigh drove back to the house.

Dear God, what else could go wrong?

"Do you think Roy contracted the flu from the Arabians?"

"I don't know," Lora Leigh said. "Only his autopsy will tell."

Hell. They'd quarantined the horses and instituted preventative measures to keep the illness from spreading, including limiting the workers' contact with the horses. But that wasn't until after Roy got sick.

He tightened his fingers on the steering wheel, his lungs aching with the effort to breathe.

Why was all this happening?

"I'll call the lab first thing in the morning and tell them about the horses so we can compare flu strains, if necessary," Lora Leigh said.

He barreled up his drive and into his garage, then threw the truck into Park. "Thank you," Flint said. "Let me know the results."

"I will."

They walked into the house, and he smelled some kind of stew Lucinda had left on the stove. But he didn't want food. He wanted a shower and a stiff drink.

Lora Leigh brushed his arm. "Flint?"

He clenched his jaw as he looked at her. "Go get cleaned up and go to bed, Lora Leigh," he said. "We'll talk tomorrow."

She stared at him for a long moment, then turned and hurried away.

He strode up to his suite, undressed and showered, then dragged on a pair of worn jeans and a shirt, not bothering to button it. Rolling his shoulders, he went back downstairs to his office, poured himself a scotch and glanced at his computer, where Lora Leigh had been searching through files when he'd found her earlier.

Suddenly, the weight of everything that had happened crashed in on him, and he downed the scotch; then he went to the window and looked out at the cloudy sky. The moon was barely a sliver of light, the stars shrouded by storm clouds.

Three of his men had been murdered. His Arabians were ill. Another employee was dead, quite possibly from the same flu that was affecting the horses.

Lora Leigh had deceived him.

And Viktor was gone forever.

His shoulders slumped, grief and worry weighing him down. And a deep loneliness clawed at his soul, making him feel physically drained.

He dropped his head forward, his shoulders shaking with the effort to control his rage and sorrow.

He was so lost in his turbulent thoughts, he didn't hear anyone approaching, but suddenly he felt a hand against his back.

"Flint?"

He closed his eyes, gritting his teeth. He had to remain strong, find out who was sabotaging him and stop it.

"What is it, Lora Leigh?"

"I'm sorry about Roy," she whispered. "And about your friend Viktor. I know you cared deeply for him."

He couldn't face her. Viktor had been like family, just as Akeem and Jackson were.

"And I'm sorry about earlier. I…was wrong not to trust you." Her voice cracked. "I know that now. That you're a good man and that you wouldn't have hurt Johnny."

Her softly spoken words were a balm to his wounded soul. He turned around, inhaled her sultry scent, saw the sincerity in her eyes, and his resistance fled. Somewhere in the back of his mind, he knew there were reasons he shouldn't touch her.

She worked for him, at least for a little while longer. And she had deceived him, had thought him capable of murder, and possibly blamed him for her father's death.

But rational thoughts fled, and he reached up and cupped her face in his hands. His heart hammered, his chest tightened, and all the pain of the past few days rose to the surface, along with the desire he'd felt when he first laid eyes on her.

Even before then, he thought silently. When he'd seen her photograph in her father's house and heard her father brag about her.

She wet her lips, her eyes darkening to violet, and his body hardened, raw passion raging through him.

"Flint…" She lifted a hand to touch his arm, and he

lowered his head and claimed her mouth with his. She tasted like sweetness and sin and…home.

A place he wanted to stay forever.

LORA LEIGH PARTED HER LIPS as Flint teased them apart with his tongue, her body humming with arousal and need.

She had come down to the kitchen for tea and had seen the light on in his office. When she'd spotted him standing at the window, looking so forlorn and alone, she'd wanted to make sure he was all right, to console him, to make amends for the pain she'd inflicted upon him. But one touch of his hands to her face and her body had burst to life with erotic sensations.

He delved deeper into her mouth, then trailed his hands down to pull her into his embrace, and she gripped his arms, clinging to him.

Her knees felt weak; her body hot and languid. Her nipples tightened beneath her robe and silk pajamas.

He kissed her tenderly at first, tentatively, but then his lips became more passionate, his hands frenzied, his breathing erratic. He moaned against her ear, his breath fanning the flames of her desire, and she slid her hands from his arms to his chest. She needed to stop this craziness now, before it went too far.

But he licked the sensitive skin behind her earlobe and slid his hand over her hip, pulling her more tightly against his rock-hard body, and instead of pushing him away, she stroked the hard planes of his chest. His skin was bronzed from the sun, his muscles were tight and thick beneath her hands, and his body was powerful and so masculine that hunger spiraled through her.

With a breathy sigh, he trailed kisses down her neck and she arched into him, her pulse racing as his thick length pulsed between her thighs.

No man had ever heated her skin to such a degree. Had ever made her want to abandon her inhibitions this way.

She pushed at his shirt until he shrugged it off; then she sucked in a breath at the sight of him.

"Lora Leigh…"

"Shh." She hushed him with a kiss, her breasts heavy and achy. As if he sensed her need, he trailed a hand down to cup her through the robe. She'd forgone the bra with her pajamas, and her nipple stiffened to a turgid peak.

A deep moan rumbled from his throat, and he kissed a path down her throat again, then lowered his hand to pull her robe apart.

She sighed his name, tingling all over as he unfastened the top button of her pajamas and his lips met her skin.

A second later, he teased her nipple with his tongue, then closed his mouth around the tip.

She sagged, clawing at his arms to steady herself but feeling as if she were melting into a molten puddle of liquid desire.

Pleasure ripped through her, and he teased her other breast with his fingers until she cried out his name. She wanted them both naked and in bed so she could pleasure him as well. So she could feel his body covering hers, his sex pulsing inside her, hear his voice calling her name as he lost himself to their coupling.

But Flint's cell phone trilled, and he tensed. Her own nerves jangled as he slowly lifted his head and looked up at her. She knew her face must be flushed, and felt wanton with her top open, her swollen breasts exposed.

The phone trilled again, and regret and worry shrouded his face as he glanced at the number.

"Do you have to answer it?" she whispered raggedly.

His eyes darkened to a feral black as his gaze fell to her breasts; then he pulled her pajama top together "Yes. That was a mistake. Go to bed, Lora Leigh."

His harsh tone felt like a slap to her face. Then he turned away and quickly connected the call, dismissing her.

Tears blurred her eyes as she fled from the room and ran up the stairs. Her body was on fire from his touch, her sex throbbing for his touch.

But he was right. That had been a mistake. One they couldn't repeat.

Confusion clouded her mind as she closed her bedroom door. In his arms, she'd forgotten the reasons they couldn't be together. The reason she'd hated him when she'd come to the Diamondback.

What would her father think if he knew she'd almost made love to their enemy? A sob of shame and…unquenched need…tore from her throat, and she lay down and curled into a ball on the plush bedding.

God help her. She was afraid she was falling for Flint McKade….

FLINT'S CHEST HEAVED, and he struggled to control his breathing as he connected the call. He wanted nothing more than to finish what he and Lora Leigh had begun. To strip her naked and take her on his desk in his office.

The detective's voice intruded on his thoughts. "McKade, you called me earlier?"

He had slipped from the stable during the foal's

delivery and made the call. "Yes, I did. It's about that guy on the plane, the one you couldn't identify."

"You think you know who he is?"

God, he hoped he was wrong. "I'm not certain, but I have an idea. I want you to have the M.E. pull dental records on a man named Johnny Whittaker."

A long pause. "Whittaker. Isn't that your vet's name?"

He reached for his shirt in disgust. "Yes. He's her brother. Apparently, he blames me for his father's suicide, because I bought his father's land. He came here to work under an assumed name, and now he's missing."

Detective Green cleared his throat. "I'll get right on it."

Flint thanked him and hung up, the memory of Lora Leigh's moans of pleasure as he'd touched her echoing in his mind.

She'd betrayed him earlier.

But now he felt as if he'd betrayed her by calling Detective Green without telling her. He only hoped he was wrong, that her brother wasn't dead. And that he wasn't responsible for the other two men's deaths.

If he died because of Flint, she'd never let him touch her again, much less forgive him.

And after that heated encounter, he wanted her more than ever.

Chapter Eleven

Flint stared at the news in disgust as he sipped his morning coffee.

"Political unrest abounds in Rasnovia," the reporter stated. "Supporters of the royal family are desolate over the family's deaths and are flocking to mass to mourn. Flowers and other offerings have been left in front of the royal palace. But armed rebel protesters have rioted, and several fires, shootings and a bombing last night have created chaos and danger for the citizens."

The camera panned to the devastation caused by a serial bomber, and Flint flipped off the set. Viktor would be upset if he could see what was happening now.

Two days had passed since he'd found Lora Leigh snooping in his office and learned that Roy Parkman had died. Lora Leigh had been avoiding him, and he'd kept his distance, the memory of their sultry kiss and how far he'd taken it haunting him.

He wanted Lora Leigh, but a personal relationship with her was impossible.

Unless he came clean and told her the truth about her father.

A truth he'd vowed not to divulge. One that might make things worse for her and compound her guilt.

Besides, he was a man of his word. Without that, his land and fortune were worthless.

And even if she knew about his deal with her dad, there was the matter of her brother....

He was still waiting on a positive ID on the third dead man, the one who might be Johnny Whittaker.

A confirmation would seal the end of any hope that Lora Leigh could forgive him and want to be with him.

Frustrated, he checked his e-mail and found one from Taylor saying there were some discrepancies in his account and that she was checking into the abnormality.

Flint frowned and made a note to follow up.

A knock sounded at the door and he tensed. "Come in."

Ortega shuffled in, rubbing at his bad leg, and Flint offered him coffee.

Ortega shook his head, his craggy features strained as he moved in front of Flint. With a scarred hand, he pushed Johnny's faxed photo across Flint's desk.

"Do you recognize him?" Flint asked.

Ortega nodded. "*Sí*. He say his name Houston."

Flint grimaced. Houston was the name on the ID found on the plane. Which meant the dead man was probably Johnny.

"He say he need job, so I let him muck stalls and do odd jobs." Ortega removed his hat and scratched his shaggy hair. "But he not show up for work in days."

"Did he say or do anything that made you suspicious?" Flint asked.

Ortega shook his head. "No, but Sanchez and Gonzalez, I found them, and they might know more."

"You think that they had something to do with the sabotage or the attack on Lora Leigh?"

"No, no, señor. They good men, work hard, only want chance," Ortega stammered.

"You're sure? Even if someone offered them more money?"

"*Sí*. One is my sister's boy, and the other my cousin's. They good. Just worry about no papers." He hesitated, then gestured toward the door. "They waiting outside. I make them come see you."

Flint nodded. "Then tell them to come in."

Ortega shifted on his good leg. "I sorry if I do wrong. I understand you want me to leave."

Flint studied the man and knew he couldn't blame him. Ortega had a good heart, and his family had suffered before Flint had hired him. Besides, with a record, he'd have trouble getting work anyplace else.

"I don't want you to leave, Ortega," Flint said. "I appreciate your hard work and dedication."

A grin slid onto the man's worried face. "Gracias, Señor Flint. Gracias."

He shuffled back outside and returned with Sanchez and Gonzalez trailing behind, their heads ducked, both looking anxious.

"Señor Flint," Gonzalez said, his English broken. "We're sorry, but we desperate for work. Please, señor, don't send us back."

Sanchez pinched the bridge of his nose, fear tightening his jaw. "*Sí*, please, señor. My family need food. My wife having niño."

Flint silently cursed. "I'm not going to send you back, but we have to arrange for your papers. I'll make a call and see what I can do."

Excitement and relief brightened the men's faces.

Flint gestured toward Johnny's photo. "Now, tell me what you know about this man."

Sanchez narrowed his eyes and pulled at his shirt. "He not work much and act—how you say—funny."

"How do you mean?" Flint asked.

Sanchez twisted his mouth, as if he was trying to figure out how to express his thoughts in English. Gonzalez piped up.

"He suspicious," Gonzalez said. "Ask about you, señor. Say bad things about you." He bit his lip. "But we tell him you good man. You give us jobs."

"What kind of bad things?" Flint asked.

Gonzalez cleared his throat but looked hesitant.

"Please," Flint said. "I need to know if he has been working against me."

Gonzalez nodded. "He say he going to destroy you."

Flint clenched his jaw. Just what he was afraid of. That Johnny might have helped set up the attack on the plane.

But if he had, why had he wound up dead?

LORA LEIGH PATTED EASTERN Promise. "Hang in there, sweetness," she said softly. "We're going to make you well."

The mare whinnied and lifted her head, then dropped it back down, and Lora Leigh sighed.

"I'm going to check with the lab today to see if they have the results of those tests I ordered. I'll be back later," she said to one of the ranch hands.

She headed into the washroom, yanked off her mask, gloves and gown, then cleaned up.

Finally, she stepped into the hot sunshine and breathed in the fresh, clean air as she climbed on Sly and rode back to the main house.

Flint was riding up to the house as she approached, his profile so ruggedly dark and masculine that her breath lodged in her throat.

She paused, tightening her fingers on the reins as he threw his long leg over the black stallion's side and slid down to the ground. He tied the horse to the wooden post by his house and patted his sleek coat.

She couldn't stand the tension between them any longer. She'd been walking on pins and needles, waiting to see if any of Flint's workers recognized Johnny and knew what had happened to him.

She gave Sly a slight kick and sent him galloping up to the house. Flint heard her approach and turned, the sun gleaming off his black hat, his chiseled jaw tight as she halted and climbed down. He immediately took the reins and tied Sly beside his horse, and for a moment, she imagined that she looked as natural beside him as Sly did beside the stallion.

Beneath the brim of his hat, his gaze pinned her as she approached.

"Is everything all right?" he asked.

"The Arabians seem to be holding their own. I haven't heard from the lab yet, but I'm heading into town."

He studied her for a long moment, his eyes somber. "I'll drive you."

Panic flared in her chest. Being alone with him in the truck seemed too intimate. She had to keep her distance until she found Johnny, then get the heck out of Flint's life.

The Diamondback was his home, his life. Not hers.

"Thanks for the offer, Flint, but I have a lunch date, so that's not necessary."

A muscle ticked in his jaw. "I'm not letting you go alone, not until we find out who's trying to hurt me and who assaulted you."

"Flint—"

"Don't argue, Lora Leigh. It's settled."

She stiffened at his high-handed tone, and a small smile curved his mouth. "I told you I'd protect you, and I intend to, whether you want me around or not."

That was the problem. She was starting to want him around all the time.

Impossible.

Even if Johnny was safe and sound, he wouldn't understand her attraction to Flint. And her daddy would roll over in his grave....

He shrugged. "Besides, I have business in town, and I need to check on my sister and nephew."

Flint strode inside to wash up, while she grabbed her purse and ran a brush through her hair, then clipped it back in a ponytail. She phoned the lab as she climbed in the truck, and the specialist she'd requested told her he'd have the results that afternoon.

"Where are you meeting your lunch date?" Flint asked in a gruff voice.

"At the Cactus Café."

"Who are you meeting?"

She smiled. "A friend."

He nodded, then retrieved his phone and made a call. "Taylor, it's me. I'll meet you at the Cactus Café in a half hour."

When he hung up, she gaped at him. "What are you doing?"

"Driving."

"You don't have to stay at the café, Flint. I'll be safe in town."

He gave her a warning look. "It's a big café, Lora Leigh. Taylor and I will sit on the opposite side and give you privacy."

Her skin prickled, her heart fluttered and she suddenly felt smothered.

Smothered but cared for in a way she hadn't been in a long time.

She breathed in his powerful scent, his anxiety, the tension palpable as they approached town.

His posture stiffened as he parked in front of the café, and they walked up to the entrance together.

He placed his hand at the back of her waist as they entered, making her feel small but feminine, then checked around the outside, as if looking to see if anyone was watching them. Did he really think someone would assault her in town?

An older, gray-haired man wearing jeans, boots and a gray Stetson suddenly blocked Flint's way. "What are you doing in here?" the man asked snidely. "Thought you only dined with the rich and famous."

"Hello, McElroy," Flint said.

The man glared at Lora Leigh with disdain, then back at Flint. "She don't look like your usual type."

"I don't have a type," Flint growled. "Don't you think it's time you get over yourself? I outbid you for Diamond Daddy fair and square."

"Money breeds money, don't it?" the bitter man said.

"And I earned every penny of mine," Flint replied coolly. "What about you?"

McElroy reared back and closed his hand into a fist, and Lora Leigh's heart raced.

"I heard you had some trouble," McElroy sneered.

"Yeah." Flint pushed his face into the other man's. "Just how much do you know about that?"

McElroy threw his head back and laughed. "Just that it serves you right for stealing Diamond Daddy from me."

"I didn't steal anything," Flint said coldly. "And if you want part of him, he's available for stud fees. But it will cost you."

McElroy's eyes glittered with pure rage. "I wouldn't pay you a dime for anything." With a loud grunt, he turned and stalked off.

Lora Leigh started to say something, but a gorgeous, young blond woman and a little boy about four, with the same light hair and blue eyes, raced over and threw themselves at Flint.

"Hey, big brother!"

"Uncle Flint, I gots a loose tooth!"

Flint swung the child up in his arms and hugged him,

and Lora Leigh melted into a gooey puddle. Seeing Flint with McElroy proved what a shrewd but tough business opponent he could be. In contrast, seeing him with his family revealed another side to the strong, tough cowboy.

Flint introduced her to them, and Taylor gave her a curious look but appeared friendly.

Lora Leigh spotted her friend Amy Gallagher across the café and waved. "That's my lunch date."

An odd look crossed Flint's face. "She's your date?"

Lora Leigh twisted sideways and froze, her blood rushing to her head. Did he think she'd come to town to meet a man? Was that the reason he'd insisted on accompanying her?

Was Flint jealous?

A nervous laugh bubbled in her throat. "Yes. Dr. Gallagher was my roommate in college and vet school."

He visibly relaxed. "I see. Have a good lunch. Just let me know when you're ready to leave."

She nodded, the tension thickening between them when she noticed the predatory gleam in his eyes, and rushed over to meet her former roommate.

Amy hugged her, and with a teasing eyebrow raised, she gestured toward Flint. "It's good to see you. How do you like working for the rich hunk?"

Lora Leigh sighed and slid down onto the seat, then took a sip of water.

"That's why I asked you to meet me," Lora Leigh said. "I'm not going to be working at the Diamondback much longer, and I wanted to give you a heads-up in case you wanted me to recommend you as my replacement."

FLINT SETTLED INTO THE seat across from Christopher and Taylor, his mind racing to keep up with Christopher's chatter.

"I wants to come to the ranch and ride Big Boy," Christopher said. "Can I, Uncle Flint?"

"Sure," Flint said, then remembered the trouble at the ranch. "But not this week, bud. Let me get some things taken care of first."

Taylor gave Flint an apologetic look. "I tried to explain, but it's hard for him to understand about your problems. He's had so many changes lately."

Flint reached out and playfully tugged at her chin, as he had when they were young. "You're doing the right thing, Taylor. I'm proud of you."

The waitress brought menus, and they ordered burgers and fries. While they waited on their food, Christopher entertained himself with a coloring sheet of a spaceship that had supposedly landed in the middle of a bed of cacti.

"Now tell me, what's going on with you?" Taylor asked.

He explained about the Arabians' symptoms and the attack on Lora Leigh.

Taylor's eyes widened. "Oh, my gosh, Flint. That's horrible."

"I know. Things are piling up."

Taylor hesitated, then squeezed his hand. "You'll get to the bottom of it, I'm sure."

"I just hope we do before anyone else gets hurt." He glanced at Lora Leigh, his stomach knotting.

"So, what exactly is going on between you and Lora Leigh?"

Flint accepted his iced tea from the waitress, then took a sip with a frown. "We work together. That's it."

Taylor winked at him. "Uh-huh. You forget you're talking to your sister. I saw the way you looked at her."

Flint shrugged. He hadn't realized he was so easy to read. "You're imagining things, sis."

Taylor laughed. "No, I'm not. You were flaming jealous because you thought she was meeting a man."

He narrowed his eyes, picked up the orange crayon Christopher had dropped and handed it back to him. "It doesn't matter. There *can't* be anything else between us, sis." He explained about buying her father's land and divulged that she and her brother both blamed him for their father's death. "And now Johnny is missing, and I'm afraid—" Flint lowered his voice so Christopher couldn't hear "—that he was killed on my plane."

Taylor scrunched her nose in a motherly, protective way, a gesture she used with her son. "She has no right to blame you for her father's death or her brother's, especially if he came to the ranch to get revenge on you."

Flint chuckled at her defensive tone. She might be smaller than him, but she'd fight tooth and nail for those she loved.

He was glad she'd left her husband to protect Christopher and herself.

"I appreciate your concern," Flint said. "But I can take care of myself."

Worried eyes met his. "You've always been the protector and hero," she said softly. "And now you're having all this trouble. I wish I could help you."

His throat thickened. "You are. You're taking care of my favorite nephew."

Christopher looked up and grinned as the food appeared, and they all dug in.

Seeing her with her son had made him want a kid of his own. He glanced up and saw Lora Leigh stand; then their gazes locked, and an intense heat rippled through him.

Lora Leigh walked toward him and stopped at the table. "Excuse me for interrupting, Flint, but Detective Green just phoned. He said he needs me to come by the station." Her face paled. "It's about Johnny."

He gripped the table edge, his heart pounding. Dammit.

If Detective Green had identified the third body on the plane as that of Johnny, her brother's death would seal his doomed fate with Lora Leigh.

LORA LEIGH'S HEART WAS hammering in her chest. Detective Green's tone had sent a chill down her spine.

Flint's sister gave her a pinched look, and she wondered if Flint had confided in her the real reason she'd come to the Diamondback. If so, Taylor must despise her.

Flint's cell phone trilled, and he glanced at it, then held up a hand. "Just a sec. It's Akeem." He removed his wallet from the pocket of his jeans. "I'll take care of the bill while I talk to him and be right back."

He stood and headed toward the register, leaving Lora Leigh alone with his sister and her son. Christopher bobbed up and down. "Can I get ice cream? Please, Mommy."

Taylor ruffled the little boy's hair with her fingers. "We'll walk to the ice-cream shop when we leave here."

"Goodie." He grinned and resumed coloring, and Taylor looked up at her.

"I'm sorry about the loss of your father," Taylor said. "I hope things work out for you."

Lora Leigh's insides twisted with nerves. She was afraid her worst fears had come true. That Johnny was dead and gone, and she was all alone.

Taylor offered a sympathetic smile and touched her hand. "Just don't blame Flint," she said softly. "It's obvious that he likes you. I've never seen him look at a woman the way he looks at you. All dark and possessive."

"He's not—"

"Yes, he is," Taylor said. "And he's a good guy, Lora Leigh. So don't hurt him."

Lora Leigh folded her arms. "How could I possibly hurt him? He has everything."

"He has money, but he's worked hard for that," Taylor said defensively. "Unfortunately, women tend to use him. They want his money, his land, not the real him."

Lora Leigh bit her lip. "I don't want his money or land," she said. "But my father…my family…"

Taylor's eyes softened with a wisdom beyond her years. "Everyone makes their own choices. Your father made his, probably because he loved you and wanted to give you the best life he could." She smiled lovingly as she looked at her son, who was chewing his bottom lip as he tried to stay in the lines of the drawing. "That's what parents do. They sacrifice for their children."

"He wouldn't have had to sell if I hadn't insisted on

college." Lora Leigh's voice broke. "He gave up everything for me."

"Because he wanted you to have your dreams." Taylor stood and squeezed her hand. "So be happy, the way he'd want you to be. And forgive yourself."

Tears burned Lora Leigh's eyes. Taylor was right. She'd blamed Flint on the surface, but the person she'd blamed the most, the one she really hated, was herself.

How could she possibly let go of that anger?

Flint returned and gave her an odd look, then glanced at Taylor. "Is everything okay?"

Lora Leigh nodded. "We need to go."

Flint guided her outside to the car. A strained expression tightened his face as they drove to the police precinct. Nausea cramped Lora Leigh's stomach as they climbed the steps to the concrete building.

Flint caught her arm before entering. "Lora Leigh…"

She blinked to control threatening tears, his sister's words echoing in her ears. *He's a good guy. I saw the way he looks at you.*

But what if the detective had uncovered evidence that Johnny had been behind the attacks on Flint and the murder of his men?

How would he feel about her then?

Chapter Twelve

Detective Green emerged from his office to usher them inside before Flint could say another word. Lora Leigh's stomach clenched at the condemning look on the detective's face.

"Come in, McKade, Dr. Whittaker."

Flint placed his hand at her waist, as he had done earlier, and Lora Leigh claimed one of the two chairs. Flint took the other, and the detective paced to the other side of his desk, his jaw set.

She crossed her leg, then folded her hands on top of her knee. "What's going on, Detective?"

His gaze cut sharply to Flint and then her, and she realized that Flint knew the reason Detective Green had called her. The hairs on the nape of her neck prickled.

He had bad news....

"I suppose McKade told you that we hadn't been able to identify one of the men who died in the plane shooting. His face was shot up pretty bad." Detective Green's voice was level, but his intense eyes bored into her own. "He was carrying a fake ID."

The first strains of panic pierced at Lora Leigh like a razor slicing through skin.

Then Detective Green spread a file in front of him and cleared his throat. "But this morning I received the autopsy report, along with an ID. Based on dental reports, we determined that the man was your brother, Dr. Whittaker."

"You're certain?" Flint asked in a gruff voice.

"Yes," Detective Green said matter-of-factly.

"No…." Lora Leigh whispered, the detective's words beating at her brain like a jackhammer. This couldn't be real. He had to be wrong.

The room spun, the light dimming, the world tilting, as if she'd fallen into a dark, empty tunnel.

Flint reached over and put his hand on her back in a comforting gesture, and Lora Leigh stiffened, then leaned forward, suddenly unable to breathe. She bowed her head into her hands. "No…no, you have to be wrong…."

"I'm sorry, Dr. Whittaker," Detective Green said quietly. "I know this comes as a shock. And I hate to do this, but I need to ask you some questions."

Tears pricked at Lora Leigh's eyes, and nausea churned through her. She needed to escape. The room was twirling again, as if she were on a free-fall ride, diving straight downward.

"The questions can wait," Flint said brusquely. He curved an arm around her. "Lora Leigh, I'm sorry. Let me take you home."

Shock, anger, desolation swept over her, and in a fog of emotions, she lashed out. "Home? I don't have a home anymore, Flint. And now, thanks to you, I don't have any family left, either."

Choking on a tortured breath, she jumped up and ran from the room, blindly searching for a way out. She spied the ladies' room, then rushed inside and dropped to her knees in one of the stalls as sobs wrenched her.

FLINT GRITTED HIS TEETH, Lora Leigh's accusations cutting him to the bone. Even though he'd prepared himself for the inevitable, hearing her actually say the words hurt more than he'd expected.

"You didn't share your suspicions before you arrived?" Detective Green asked.

Flint flexed his hands. "I was hoping we were wrong."

"Did you talk to your employees about Whittaker?"

"Yes," Flint said, hating to impugn Lora Leigh's brother. But he had to know the truth. "Two of the men said that he acted strange, that he was bad-mouthing me and nosing around about my business."

"He had a grudge against you?"

Flint reluctantly nodded. "He blamed me for his father's death because I bought the Double W from his father right before he killed himself."

Detective Green's eyes flattened with suspicion. "I see. Then it's possible he helped set up the sabotage?"

"I guess it's possible," Flint admitted. "But don't accuse him of that in front of Lora Leigh unless you have evidence."

"You don't think he told Lora Leigh what he was up to?"

Flint chewed the inside of his cheek.

"McKade, did she know what he was up to?"

"She knew he came to the ranch to get back at me," Flint said. "But no specifics."

"And you believe her?" Detective Green asked in an incredulous voice.

Did he trust Lora Leigh?

"Yes," he said. And if her brother had planned the sabotage, he couldn't blame her for his actions.

Flint stood, hands fisted by his sides. "If that's it, I'm going to check on her."

Detective Green scowled. "Actually, there is something else. We examined your financial records and found some discrepancies. You failed to mention that you set up fake accounts. Are you hiding money for tax purposes?"

Flint frowned, anger slamming into him. "I don't know what you're talking about."

Detective Green arched a thick brow. "Paperwork shows you also took out extra insurance on the Arabians."

Pure rage burned through Flint at his implications, and he slapped his hand on the desk. "That's a lie. I pride myself on working ethically and fairly. I don't have fake accounts, and I certainly would never endanger any animal to make a buck. Someone, the same person who set up the attack at the airport, must have hacked into my files. Don't you see, they're trying to ruin me?"

Detective Green's cold, condemning gaze pierced him. "Maybe, maybe not. But I will get to the truth, McKade. Neither your anger nor Dr. Whittaker's tears will stop me."

"When you find the truth, let me know," Flint snarled. "And then you'll owe me an apology."

Furious, he turned and stalked out the door, his boots pounding the floor as he went to search for Lora Leigh.

He spotted her exiting the ladies' room, her complexion ashen, her eyes gaunt. Sympathy welled in his chest, but her last comment to him before she'd run from the room stung.

Still, she was grief stricken and needed someone to lean on. And he had to offer her his shoulder.

GRIEF CRAWLED THROUGH Lora Leigh, threading its deep roots all the way to her soul. She stumbled from the restroom, uncertain what to do now or where to go.

She felt lost, alone, as if she had no one to turn to.

And then she spotted Flint in the hallway, larger than life, more masculine and stronger than any man had a right to be. She made a low sound in her throat. She knew the questions Detective Green had intended to ask. She just didn't know the answers.

And the truth terrified her.

Her gaze locked with his, and she trembled. Flint must hate her.

She had blamed him for her brother's death, when she knew that Johnny's own sick need for revenge had set him on the course that had led to his demise. Yet, somehow her throat was too clogged with sorrow and pain to formulate an apology.

She rubbed a hand over her face, swiping at tears that wouldn't stop spilling from her eyes, and wished she could bury herself beneath her grandmother's thick quilts, feel her comforting arms and hear her soothing voice. But she was gone, too.

Flint strode to her, his powerful shoulders pulled back, the dark beard stubble of his permanent five o'clock shadow adding to the intimidating cowboy image that made women swoon. She braced herself for bitter words of retaliation, but he shocked her by reaching out and pulling her into his arms. She stiffened at first, knowing she didn't deserve his comfort or forgiveness, yet his wide hands stroked her back and her chest heaved against him, a pent-up breath escaping.

"I'm so sorry, Lora Leigh," he whispered into her hair.

His generous gesture touched her so deeply she shuddered against him. "I…"

"Shh, it's okay. You don't have to say anything."

She nodded helplessly against his chest, his breath fanning her cheek as he continued to hold her. He soothed her, stroking her back and whispering soft words of comfort.

And Lora Leigh fell deeply in love with the man.

So deeply she thought she was drowning.

He held her for what seemed like an eternity. From somewhere in the distance drifted the drone of voices and telephones, the elevator dinged, footsteps pounded, but anyone else might as well have been a million miles away.

Finally, her shoulders stopped shaking, and she swallowed back another river of tears threatening to overflow. Struggling for composure, she took a deep breath, inhaling his musky odor and implanting it in her memory forever.

When she tilted her chin up to look at him, the compassion in his eyes nearly brought her to her knees. Of course, he understood grief. He'd just buried his best friend.

And two of his men.

Maybe because of her brother.

"I have to see him," she whispered hoarsely.

His eyes darkened to black coals. "I don't think that's a good idea, Lora Leigh."

"Why not?" she asked, but as soon as she muttered the question, she understood the reason for his protest. "You saw him, didn't you? And he looks bad…."

Regret twisted the angular planes of his face. "Yes." He brushed her hair from her forehead with his thumb. "Trust me. That's not the way you want to remember him."

She squeezed her eyes closed, willing away the grisly images her imagination had magically produced. But resolve set in, and she knew she'd never have closure, never trust that he was gone, until she held his hand and said goodbye.

"I need to do this," she said, her voice stronger than she'd thought possible. "I have to see him for myself to know that it's really him."

A tense heartbeat of a second passed between them. "But you won't recognize him. His face…was shot."

Fresh grief and rage flooded her throat. "I'll know," she said, straightening herself and summoning her strength. "Will you drive me, or should I find a way to go myself?"

Regret softened his expression. "All right. I'll take you. I won't let you go through this alone."

Lora Leigh leaned into him as he guided her to his truck. As soon as she buried Johnny and found the truth, she would leave the Diamondback and stand on her own.

Flint's ranch would always symbolize the home and family she had lost.

If only she'd stopped her brother from coming to the Diamondback, none of this would have happened. He'd be alive and well, and some day maybe their hatred for Flint and their grief for their father would have dissolved.

Now any hope of that was lost forever....

BRINGING LORA LEIGH to the morgue was a mistake, Flint thought as they entered the sterile concrete building. She shuddered beside him, and he drew her into the crook of his arm, offering her support as they walked down the long, cold hallway. The scent of formaldehyde and other chemicals assaulted him, the kind of acrid odors that sank into a person's skin and throat and hair and could never be washed away.

Long-buried memories rose to the surface like hands clawing at him, forcing him to remember the day his parents had died.

He'd been sixteen and filled with teenage contempt for his father. Had berated him for not wanting a place of his own, for being content to earn wages from another man's profit.

God, he'd been stupid. As he'd stood in the morgue and stared at the blank, sightless eyes of his mother and father on steel slabs, he'd broken down like a baby and begged his father for forgiveness.

Still, he had wanted land of his own, had needed to feel his fingers on the pulse of the business, his hands in the dirt, his own butt in the saddle, working the animals that belonged to him. He still prayed his father understood that he loved him and respected him for all he'd given him.

The sound of Lora Leigh's labored breathing drew him back from the depths of his own turbulent past. They met the medical examiner, Dr. Parrish, in his office. With thick, patchy tufts of white hair and a beard, he was in his sixties and had worked at this same morgue for years. Judging from the glint in his steely-gray eyes, he remembered Flint as well.

Flint introduced him to Lora Leigh.

"Detective Green told me that you identified my brother," Lora Leigh said.

Dr. Parrish glanced at Flint, then clasped his hands over Lora Leigh's. "Yes, I did. I'm sorry for your loss, Dr. Whittaker."

Lora Leigh bit down on her lip and gave a shaky nod. "I'd like to see him."

This elicited another concerned look from Dr. Parrish, and Flint shrugged. "I advised her not to, but she insists."

"I'm a doctor," Lora Leigh said, with conviction. "I can handle it. I have to say goodbye."

"All right," Dr. Parrish said gently. "We can do it via screen if you prefer."

"No, I want to…see him in person. It's the only way I'll have closure."

Dr. Parrish's bushy white brows rose, but he gestured for her to follow him. Flint stayed close behind her, again wanting to offer her privacy yet determined to be supportive.

When they stepped into the room, the smell of death and chemicals swirled around him, and he coughed, but Lora Leigh didn't seem to notice. She zeroed in on the body on the steel slab, then walked slowly over to it. Dr. Parrish accompanied her and lifted the sheet from the body.

A soft gasp of pain reverberated from Lora Leigh; then she bravely pulled herself together. Flint's heart squeezed as she picked up the young man's hand and examined it.

When she glanced at Flint, tears glistened in her eyes like huge diamonds. "It's him. He got that scar when he was ten and whittling with my father."

Flint hated the sound of pain in her voice, but he didn't know how to help her.

She traced a finger over Johnny's shattered jaw, then bent and kissed the palm of his hand.

"What happened, Johnny?" she whispered. "I wish you were here and could tell me."

Flint vowed to find the answers and give them to her. He only hoped the truth wouldn't hurt her more than her brother's death already had.

MEMORIES FLOODED LORA Leigh in a blinding rush. Johnny playing Little League and hitting the winning run when he was ten. Johnny pulling her pigtails and putting worms in her bed. She and Johnny racing across the Double W on horseback, then wading in the creek and watching their father break the new horses he brought to the ranch.

She kissed Johnny's hand one last time, her heart aching. If only she'd stopped him from seeking revenge, he'd still be alive. And together they might have found a way to buy the Double W back from Flint.

Determined not to fall apart again, she pulled herself together and thanked the medical examiner, then told him she'd be in touch about arrangements for a funeral service.

Flint followed her outside, and she paused to inhale the fresh air and sunshine, trying desperately to banish the acrid scent of death and chemicals.

Flint was right. Johnny hadn't looked like himself. His face had been grotesque; his skin and bones shattered; his right eye socket sagging. As a doctor, she'd learned to compartmentalize, and her medical instincts had kicked in, saving her.

But as his big sister, she would be haunted by the image forever.

Flint pressed his hand to her waist for support. "Are you all right?" he asked.

She shook her head. Her family was all gone.

She'd never be all right again.

Chapter Thirteen

As soon as they arrived back at the ranch, Lora Leigh rushed up the steps.

Flint followed her, his muscles taut with tension. She hadn't spoken on the way back to his house, but he could see the wheels of panic racing in her head.

She hurried into her suite, and he knocked, then opened the door. She jerked her suitcase from the closet, then started tossing clothes inside it. Jeans, shirts, underwear.

Very sexy lacy bras and panties, which made his body harden as desire rippled through him.

"What are you doing?" he asked.

"Packing. I'm going to move into town."

"Why?"

"I can't stay here, Flint. Not after today…"

"You're not going anywhere, Lora Leigh. It's not safe. Not until we find out who attacked you."

Fear flashed in her eyes at the memory, but she quickly masked it. "You can't want me here now. Not with your suspicions about Johnny."

"We don't know anything for certain, Lora Leigh."

"No…" Her voice cracked. "But even if he did do something wrong, Flint, he was my brother, and I loved him."

Flint hated the pain in her voice but fisted his hands at his sides to keep from reaching for her. "I understand that. And I wouldn't be a very big man if I blamed you for whatever he may or may not have done."

An odd look flickered in her eyes; then she glanced up at him with such a tormented look that he closed the distance between them.

"I'm sorry for what I said earlier, Flint. That wasn't fair." Grief and pain twisted her face as she dropped her head forward and reached for another shirt. "I was just so upset."

He knew the apology cost her. "Forget it."

She stuffed several tank tops in with the other clothing. "That friend of mine, the one I had lunch with," she said in a trembling voice. "She's interested in working for you. If you want me to call her and set up a meeting, I will."

Flint frowned. "I don't need another full-time vet."

She glanced up at him with a tremulous look. "I meant as my replacement."

His eyes darkened. "I don't want a replacement, Lora Leigh," he said gruffly. "I want you."

"Flint…" Her gaze met his, her face crumpling.

Hunger and passion spiraled through him, as well as the need to comfort her.

Unable to resist, he pulled her into his arms and pressed her head against his chest, then stroked her back. His chest heaved at the sound of her labored breathing.

"Please, Lora Leigh. The horses need you." He lowered his voice to a whisper. "And so do I."

Lora Leigh sagged in his arms, her breath a whisper against his chest as she buried her head in the crook of his arm. "How can you say that? How can you be so forgiving?"

He kissed the top of her head and rubbed slow circles between her shoulder blades. "Because I'm drawn to you, Lora Leigh. Can't you feel this connection, this fire between us?"

She slowly lifted her face, and his chest clenched when he saw the tears glittering on her eyelashes. "I'm drawn to you, too. But it's wrong…."

He shook his head firmly. "How can it be wrong when it feels so right?"

Their gazes locked, and she lifted one hand to cup his cheek, stirring a raw, aching hunger in him that only she could sate. His breath quickened, and she parted her lips on a sultry sigh of submission.

All reason fled, and he lowered his mouth and claimed her lips with his. She stroked his jaw, coaxing him to deepen the kiss, and he teased her lips apart with his tongue and slipped inside to taste her.

One taste and a raging fire lit his body, heating his blood and arousing his baser instincts. The past few days had been hell for both of them, and he wanted to alleviate her pain and fear.

His kiss became more demanding, his hands trailing over her shoulders and breasts, searching, teasing, urging her to let him love her.

An image of the underwear he'd seen her stuff in her

suitcase taunted him, and an urgency to see what color Lora Leigh was wearing now seized him. He reached for the hem of her blouse, desperate to touch her bare skin and give her pleasure, but a knock sounded on the door and she stiffened.

"Dr. Whittaker," Lucinda called. "Are you in there?"

Flint silently cursed, then held up a hand. "Let me take care of whatever it is."

He walked to the door and opened it. "Yes, Lucinda?"

A startled expression glimmered in Lucinda's eyes. "*Sí*, señor. A detective…Green, he say he need to see Dr. Whittaker."

Flint grimaced. "All right. Thank you, Lucinda. We'll be right down."

He glanced at Lora Leigh, his heart pounding. She was clutching her hands together, but the passion that had brightened her color a second ago was gone, and fear and sorrow had returned to haunt her.

LORA LEIGH INHALED SHARPLY, desperate to regain her composure before facing the detective. Although part of her yearned to stay inside the safety of the room. Inside the warm circle of Flint's arms.

For whatever Detective Green had to tell her might be the final straw.

God…Johnny. Her baby brother was dead. Gone forever.

Flint massaged the back of her neck. "Lora Leigh, I'll tell him to come back tomorrow."

She shook her head and swiped at her eyes. "No, I have to know the reason he's here."

He steadied her with a hand to her waist, and she gathered her courage like a blanket around her shoulders and walked down the steps. Detective Green was waiting in Flint's office, his tie askew, his white shirt rumpled.

"McKade," Detective Green said, with a clipped nod. "Dr. Whittaker."

Lora Leigh wanted to stand and face him, but her knees felt jittery, so she sank into a leather chair and knotted her hands.

"What are you doing here?" Flint asked, without preamble.

Detective Green's gaze cut to her. "I went by your brother's apartment in town and found some interesting things."

"What?" Lora Leigh asked.

The detective laid a notebook on the desk and opened it. "Pages of notations about destroying Flint McKade."

Lora Leigh trembled. "Does he say anything specific?"

Flint leaned over the desk and flipped through the pages. "That he hates me. Blames me for your father's death." He glanced up at her. "That he wanted to find dirt on me to ruin my reputation."

"Planning an attack on your shipment of Arabians would do the trick," Detective Green suggested. "And it does look like he was the one who tampered with your financial records."

Lora Leigh wanted to argue but couldn't. "The computer sabotage sounds like Johnny, but I can't believe he'd murder anyone, much less attack animals. He loved the ranch as much as my father and I did."

Detective Green made a sound in his throat, then

removed a sheet of paper from his inside pocket. "Really? Because we checked his phone records, both his landline and cell phone. There were several calls to your Middle Eastern contact, Amal Jabar."

Flint shifted. "That might not be anything. Johnny helped transport the Arabians from the quarantine center to the airport and flew with them. It makes sense that he might have contacted Jabar."

"You're defending him," Detective Green said, with a surprised look.

Flint shrugged. "Just trying to get to the truth and consider all options."

Detective Green grunted. "Whatever. But I want to question Jabar myself. He's still not answering my calls, and that's enough to make me suspicious."

"I'll see if I can get in touch with him," Flint said. "But I don't see Jabar endangering the horses. And as far as I know, he's never had a beef with me."

Detective Green scratched his head. "Maybe Johnny just used Jabar for information. Or maybe they collaborated, and Jabar has disappeared because he knows we're on to them."

Lora Leigh shook her head again. "Johnny wouldn't hurt anyone. I know it."

"His notations prove he was out of control and full of rage," Detective Green said, dismissing her protests. "With that combination, how can you be certain what he'd do?"

Lora Leigh picked at a loose thread on the hem of her blouse. Johnny *had* been desperate…. "I just know he's never been violent before."

"Drugs and booze can change a man," Detective Green said.

"Let's just say for a minute that it wasn't Johnny," Flint said. "What other motive could someone have if the attack wasn't meant to sabotage me?"

Detective Green shrugged. "Like I mentioned before, it could be some kind of a smuggling operation, and things went awry."

Flint frowned. "But Jabar has worked with me for years and is financially well off. I can't see him getting involved in anything like smuggling."

"Just get in touch with him so we can talk to him," Detective Green said. "Maybe he can give us some answers." He glanced at Lora Leigh. "And maybe he can tell us exactly what your brother was up to."

THE NEXT TWO DAYS, FLINT sensed that Lora Leigh was holding on to her control by a fraying thread. In addition to treating the horses, she had planned a small memorial service for her brother.

He met her at the bottom of the stairs and was disturbed by the dark purple smudges beneath her eyes, which were accentuated by her pale complexion and her stark black sundress. He had heard her crying twice during the night and had wanted to go to her, but he'd also heard her lock the door, erecting a barrier between them.

One he didn't know how to breach.

"I'll drive you," he said quietly.

She met his gaze, her sorrow tearing at him. "Thank you, but Amy is picking me up in a minute."

The doorbell rang, and she rushed past him. "That's probably her now."

Lucinda had reached the door and greeted the young woman, who offered Flint a warm smile. This was the woman Lora Leigh had met in town, the one she was grooming as her replacement.

"Flint, this is Dr. Amy Gallagher," Lora Leigh said as she ushered her into the foyer.

He extended his hand. "It's nice to meet you, Dr. Gallagher."

"The pleasure is all mine," Amy said.

"I was just telling Lora Leigh that I'll be happy to drive her. That goes for both of you."

"I don't think that's a good idea, not under the circumstances," Lora Leigh said curtly.

Her friend glanced at her, then back at him, with a concerned shrug. "Don't worry. I'll take good care of her."

He gave her a clipped nod, although his gaze followed Lora Leigh as she walked out the door. He had to do something.

Find out the truth about what was happening so he and Lora Leigh could move on with their lives.

Although he'd like for them to move on together.

But that seemed impossible.

Deciding to investigate on his own, he went to the office, then punched in Akeem's number. "It's Flint. Have you been able to get in touch with Jabar?"

"I'm afraid not," Akeem said. "I've left messages with all my contacts and his people, too. His assistant said he's in Turkey on business, and she's left messages for him to call back."

"Dammit," Flint said. "I need to find out what Johnny Whittaker was up to. And Detective Green insinuated that Amal might have been smuggling something. I can't believe that's true."

"No, neither can I," Akeem said.

"I know you trust him," Flint said. "And I'm not doubting you, Akeem. I just want to get to the bottom of this."

"I'll let you know as soon as I hear from Jabar."

"Thanks." He hung up and rubbed the back of his neck as Lora Leigh's face flashed into his mind. She was at her brother's funeral service now.

If Johnny had known the truth about his father and the reason he'd sold Flint the ranch, would he have felt differently? Would he have still wanted revenge?

Or would he have gone on with his life?

He dropped his head into his hands. What a mess. And all because of lies. Lies and a secret that he had vowed to keep because of an old man's pride.

LORA LEIGH DABBED HER EYES with a tissue as she dropped the rose petals on Johnny's tombstone. The late afternoon sunshine scorched her back, the scent of flowers sweetening the balmy air. It was too beautiful a day to bury anyone, much less to say goodbye.

Several of Johnny's friends approached her and offered condolences, along with her friends from vet school who'd heard of her loss.

"I'm sorry about Johnny," Dr. Murdock said. "Such a tragedy for him to die so young. But he's with your father now."

Her throat closed. Robert Murdock and her father had been friends for years. He'd delivered both her and Johnny and nursed them through childhood diseases, and he'd overseen her mother's medical care when she was diagnosed with cancer.

"Let me know if you need anything," he said solemnly.

She nodded, then said goodbye to a few other visitors, and the crowd dwindled.

Amy patted her shoulder. "Are you okay?"

How could she be okay when everyone she'd ever loved had died? "Just give me a few minutes. I'd like to visit with my dad."

"I'll wait by the car," Amy said.

"Thanks. I won't be long." Lora Leigh knelt between her parents' graves and Johnny's, images of her childhood returning in bittersweet snippets. She and Johnny competing in sack races across the pasture. Playing horseshoes in the backyard. Pulling grape tomatoes from their mother's tomato vines, then dipping them in water and popping them into their mouths.

Memories of Johnny's childish pranks followed. The time when he'd taken his BB gun and shot holes in the cucumbers on the vines. Johnny hiding a frog in her lunch box to scare her. Johnny hiding in the backseat of her teenage boyfriend's car and tagging along on their date. Her father teaching Johnny how to ride his first bike. The two of them going to the monster truck rally or hiking in the woods.

Johnny leaning on her at her father's funeral, vowing to get revenge on Flint.

"Oh, Johnny, what did you do?"

She angrily wiped at her tears, lost as to what to do.

Time lapsed into a surreal state as the grave diggers covered her brother's grave with dirt, then spread the flowers people had sent across the top.

"I'm so sorry I let you down," she whispered. "But I promise I won't now. If you're innocent, I'll make sure everyone knows."

And if he wasn't… She wouldn't allow herself to go down that road.

Finally, as the last strains of sunlight faded on the horizon, she forced herself to walk back to the car. Amy was waiting beneath a shade tree and drove her back to the ranch.

Lora Leigh slipped inside the main house, not wanting to see Flint, then changed into jeans and a T-shirt, grabbed the pistol he'd given her and hurried down the stairs to her Jeep. She needed to be alone, to ride across the land and feel the spring air on her face.

She also wanted to look in on the horses while she was out.

She rode as far as the fence allowed, savoring the sounds of the ranch and the fresh air. She paused to watch a blue heron take flight, then to study the whistling ducks. Deer ran freely in the hills, and one of the feral pigs Flint had told her about raced into a cluster of bushes.

A cactus wren caught her eye as she started back, and she silently admitted that Flint's environmental vision and care of the land and wildlife deserved recognition. If anything, he'd sacrificed useable ranch land and farmland to preserve endangered species. She finally understood why the articles about him in the press had hailed him as a leader in the industry.

Dark was descending as she headed back to the main house, casting the land in a gray hue, making the prickly cacti and natural habitat appear wild and untamed.

And reminding her of Flint.

This was his land. His home.

Not hers.

Although, for a brief second, she admitted that she was beginning to love the Diamondback and all that Flint had done to preserve the environment and animal life.

She massaged her temple.

But, she couldn't love Flint or his ranch. Loving them meant betraying her father and brother.

Suddenly, a noise startled her, and she peered to the left and thought she saw a shadow sneaking past the fence. Alarm immediately rippled up her spine, and she nudged Sly forward, then heard footsteps, rocks tumbling and a rush of cattle stampeding the land.

Remembering that Flint had said the fence had been cut before and that Tate had tried to steal cattle, she turned the horse and sped back toward the main house. But as she bypassed the broodmare barn, a streak of orange caught her eye.

She pulled back on the reins and patted Sly, urging him to slow down. The orange glow shot into the inky sky, growing brighter as she approached, and a plume of smoke rolled upward in a gray fog.

God, no… The stable housing the quarter horses was on fire.

Chapter Fourteen

"Listen, Flint, I didn't have anything to do with the shooting on your plane or that Whittaker guy's death." Tate staggered toward his ratty sofa and collapsed, then took another swig of beer. "Now get the hell out."

Flint studied his so-called brother, thinking he was pathetic and a jerk, but he seriously doubted Tate had the brains or guts to orchestrate a hit on his plane. He seemed to lean toward petty crimes, like cutting fences and trying to rustle cattle, and he hadn't even been good at that.

Besides, Flint had snuck a hair from Tate's brush to have tested and received a call this afternoon with DNA results. Tate was not his father's child.

"If I find out you did," Flint growled, "I'll hunt you down like a dog and haul you in to the cops myself."

Tate glared at him with bleary, hate-filled eyes, then leaned over and spit on Flint's boot. Flint cursed and grabbed Tate's shirt collar, then jerked him up to his raised fist.

Tate's eyes suddenly widened, and Flint realized he

was nothing more than a coward with a big mouth. Hell, he wasn't worth it.

His creed of ethics kicked in, and he simply shoved Tate back onto the sofa with a warning. "Stay away from me and my property. I heard from the lab, and you're not a McKade, after all. So go find your real daddy, and leave me the hell alone."

Tate's face blanched in surprise, and Flint realized the guy hadn't known. But hopefully, the truth would steer him away from causing any more trouble for him.

He turned and headed toward the door, but his cell phone vibrated against his hip. He checked the number, and a knot of anxiety gripped his insides.

His pulse racing, he quickly hit Redial and was rewarded by a voice. "Lora Leigh?"

"Flint, the stable housing the quarter horses is on fire! I called nine-one-one."

"Call for the ranch hands. Don't you dare go inside."

But the sound of wood popping and crackling echoed across the line; then the phone went dead.

Either she hadn't heard him or she was already halfway inside when she called. Dammit. Lora Leigh might hate him, but she'd raced in to save his horses at the expense of her own life.

LORA LEIGH PATTED SLY and sent him galloping away to safety. Smoke curled upward from the burning roof, rising into the sky, and orange flames shot skyward in jagged lines against the darkness.

She raced to the stable door and heard the horses whinnying, kicking and pawing wildly.

She had to save them. She couldn't leave them in there to die. And if she waited on the fire truck, they wouldn't survive.

Sweat beaded on her lip as she pressed her hand to the door. It was warm but not hot yet, so maybe she had time.

Heat scalded her neck as she inched inside, her eyes scanning the stable to locate the hot spots. God, how was she going to get all the animals out in time?

There were forty stalls, twenty on each side. Thankfully, none of them were ablaze yet. The roof crackled, and flames shot through the hayloft where the fire had obviously started. Fiery patches had popped up in three places on the floor where a loose board had fallen, and the flames were starting to spread.

The horses kicked, their hoofs pounding the wooden stall doors as they tried to escape. "I'm here now," she said gently. "I'll get you out."

She raced to the back, trying to calm the first horse as she slid back the latch on the stall door and released him. The stallion galloped past her, racing into the clearing outside. Smoke began to fog the stable, and she coughed as she hurried to the next stall.

"Shh, it's all right," she said as the horse pawed madly at the floor. She continued to murmur to him as she opened the stall door, but the big animal panicked and stepped backward, cowering against the wall. She slowly approached him, speaking softly, urging him to come to her. "Come on, baby. We have to get you out of here."

Fire hissed and spit, flames shooting sparks across the stable floor, catching in other patches. She grabbed a rope, slid it around the gelding's neck and coached him out of the stall, then led him through the fog of smoke.

The smoke was thickening and the flames were licking at her feet as she raced to the next stall and unlatched its door.

She had to hurry.

One, two, three, four, five, she opened the stall doors, then jumped aside as the horses nearly stampeded her in their rush to escape. "Go!" she shouted, then ran to the next one. But the stallion was skittish, and flames were dancing inside the stall, chewing at the wood.

"It's okay. I'm not going to leave you." She grabbed a blanket and slapped at the hissing flames, then threw it on the floor and stomped out the flames closest to the horse. Smoke clogged her lungs, and she coughed, then slapped the horse on its hindquarters, urging him to go.

Just as she made it past the stall, wood splintered and cracked from the roof, raining down. She ducked, covering her head with her hands as it ignited the wood shavings covering the floor of the stall. But another piece of wood caught her by surprise; it slammed into her head and sent her pitching to the floor.

Heat suffused her, along with smoke, but she rolled to her hands and knees to reach the next stall, then unlatched its door. The stallion bucked, rearing and making a frightened noise. "Go on, Smoky!" she ordered.

The fire was raging now, wood and shavings being eaten by the flames. She felt weak and disoriented and tried to crawl forward but collapsed as another burning board soared down and landed beside her.

No…she couldn't pass out. Then who would save the rest of the animals?

FLINT'S HEART POUNDED AS HE spotted the burning stable. Flames leaped toward the sky, wood cracked and popped, and smoke swirled in a blinding haze. Two of his quarter horses darted from the blaze in wild panic and raced toward the east.

Dear God, he hoped Lora Leigh wasn't trapped in there, trying to save his stock.

He swung the truck to the left side, away from the wind and smoke, threw the vehicle into Park and jumped out. Jake Kenner and two of his ranch hands rode up in Jake's Range Rover and climbed out, rushing toward him.

"Help me get the horses out!" Flint shouted. "I think Lora Leigh's inside. I'm going to find her."

He took a deep breath before rushing inside, the heat immediately taking his breath away and burning his face. Jake and his ranch hands ran in right behind him.

"Lora Leigh! Where are you?" Flint yelled. Sweat beaded on his skin as he hunkered low, pulled his handkerchief from his pocket to cover his mouth and crept forward, dodging fiery patches. The horses were stomping, the fire thundering louder. "Lora Leigh! Tell me where you are."

A hoarse whisper echoed from the right. "Over here."

Relief flooded him. She was alive.

He jogged toward the back, jumping over patches of fire eating the building. By the time he plowed through the smoke, she was pulling herself forward by the rail. Soot and dirt stained her face, and she coughed madly.

He knelt beside her and pushed a sweat-soaked strand of hair from her cheek. "Are you all right?"

She nodded but had to shout over the roaring blaze. "Yes, but we have to get the rest of the animals out."

He grabbed her around the waist, and she leaned on him, then a burning board sailed down and landed on the floor beside them. "My men are here now. They'll get them. I'm taking you outside."

"But Flint—"

"Don't argue," he yelled. "You need fresh air."

He led her forward, dodging burning debris and wood, relieved to see Jake and his men releasing the remaining horses. Once they finally stepped from the fire pit, he coaxed Lora Leigh a good distance away from the stable. She leaned against him, coughing and gasping for air as he urged her to sit down beneath a giant oak.

Sirens roared, and a fire engine sped down the graveled road and screeched to a halt. Then firefighters jumped off the truck and vaulted into action.

He pressed his hand to her cheek. "Stay here. I'll be right back."

She nodded and slumped against the massive tree trunk, looking small and pale but so damn beautiful and brave that he hated to leave her. The stable roof crackled, caving in, the wooden structure erupting into flames.

One of the firemen jogged toward him. "Any injuries so far?"

"No, but she could use some oxygen."

"What happened?"

"I don't know, but it could be arson. I'm calling the police."

The fireman gave a short nod, then went and retrieved the oxygen for Lora Leigh.

Flint phoned Detective Green. "Listen, I've got trouble. One of my stables is on fire."

"You suspect it was intentionally set?" Detective Green asked.

"In light of everything else, hell yeah."

"Your half brother?"

"Tate isn't my half brother," Flint growled. "And, no, it's not him this time. I was with him when I got the call."

"All right," Green mumbled. "I'll be right out."

The next few hours were chaos. Flint sent his men to round up the panicked horses and secure them so they could be checked for injuries and smoke inhalation, while the firemen worked to extinguish the flames and kept the fire from spreading.

Lora Leigh walked toward him, a blanket around her shoulders, her face pale and smudged with soot. "Flint?"

His pulse hammered at the memory of her on the floor in the midst of the raging fire. She could have died... "I'm going to have one of my men drive you back to the house."

"I need to examine the horses once you round them up."

He shook his head, his anger and frustration at the boiling point. He could tolerate losing a stable, but knowing he'd almost lost ten good horses—and Lora Leigh—was making him crazy.

Who hated him so damn much?

"I'll have one of the other vets do that. You need to get some rest."

"I'm fine, Flint. And I don't mind—"

"I said no."

Lora Leigh curled her fingers around his arm, and Flint gestured to Jake. "Jake, please take Dr. Whittaker back to the main house."

"Sure, boss."

But Detective Green strode toward them with raised brows, and cut off her departure.

"You were here when the fire started?" he asked Lora Leigh.

She shook her head. "No, I was out riding and saw smoke, so I headed this way."

The detective gestured toward the stable. "Did you see anyone nearby?"

She frowned and tugged the blanket around her shoulders. "No, although, come to think of it, I thought I saw a shadow, someone, up around the northeastern cattle pasture. But it was dark, and I couldn't be sure."

"Could have been the person who set the fire getting away," mused Detective Green.

"You think it was arson?" Lora Leigh asked.

Flint cleared his throat. "I asked him to check into that possibility."

She lifted her chin in defiance toward the detective. "Well, this time you can't blame my brother."

Flint swallowed, watching the smoke roll across the sky in ominous clouds. "Did you find anything, Detective?"

"The fire chief said they smelled traces of an accelerant. When the fire dies down and it's safe, we'll get a crime scene unit out here to investigate and take samples."

Detective Green glanced up at Jake Kenner. "Did you see anything?"

Jake shook his head. "No, I was in the bunkhouse when Mr. McKade called."

"We should question your other hands," Detective Green said.

Flint rubbed the back of his neck. He didn't intend to let Detective Green harass Lora Leigh. "If you're finished with them," Flint said, "I want Jake to take Lora Leigh back to the main house. She risked her life to save my stock."

Detective Green twisted his mouth. "I'm done with them for now. But if you think of anything, call me."

"I'll see you back at the house," Lora Leigh said.

Flint cut his eyes toward her. He wanted to go with her, to hold her so badly he could barely breathe. "Definitely. But don't wait up. It's going to be a long night."

Although he wished that when he got home, he could crawl into bed with her.

LORA LEIGH STRIPPED AND stepped into the shower, leaning her head back as the warm water sluiced over her bare skin. Images of the stable collapsing into flames and the terrified horses haunted her, and she shivered.

What if she'd been too late?

No, she couldn't think like that. But someone definitely wanted to hurt Flint, to destroy his ranch and make him suffer.

She had the insane urge to find the person who'd set that fire and strangle them herself. Flint didn't deserve this.

Yet hadn't she come to the Diamondback for revenge herself?

Shame washed over her, and she soaped her hair and

body, scrubbing her hair twice to erase the smoky scent, but it lingered in her mind, a horrifying memory.

What a hell of a day. The funeral for Johnny. Her visit to her parents' graves. The fire and panicked horses.

Flint rushing in, his features strained with worry.

Finally, when the water grew cool, she climbed out and dried off, then slipped on a pair of short cotton tap pants, a camisole and a cotton robe. Antsy, she went down to the den and paced, wondering how long Flint would be. If he'd found a clue to indicate who'd set the fire.

What if the person out to destroy Flint had stayed around to watch? To go after him once everyone else left?

Lucinda poked her head into the room. "Do you need anything, Señorita Lora Leigh? Some dinner? Tea?"

She just needed to know Flint was back and that he was all right. "Tea would be great," Lora Leigh said, suddenly chilled.

Lucinda nodded and returned a few minutes later with a tray. She started to pour the tea, but Lora Leigh wasn't accustomed to being waited on, so she reached for the pot, but her hand was shaking.

"Rest. You have been through much," said Lucinda. She smiled and patted her arm, then took over the task and handed the cup to Lora Leigh.

"Thank you, Lucinda," Lora Leigh said.

"*Sí*," Lucinda said with a worried look. "Was anyone hurt tonight?"

"Thankfully, no."

"So Señor Flint is all right?"

Lora Leigh added sweetener to the tea and took a sip. "Yes. He was talking to the detective when I left.

We rescued all the horses, but I'm afraid the stable is a total loss."

Lucinda crossed herself, murmuring something in Spanish, which Lora Leigh assumed was a prayer of thanks that no one was injured, then left the room.

Lora Leigh curled up on the sofa and sipped the hot tea, physically and emotionally drained. Grief mounted as the night wore on, and she thought about Johnny and her father.

Her anxiety for Flint grew as well. She couldn't rest until he returned, although guilt assaulted her for caring about him.

Finally, fatigue claimed her, and she fell asleep on the sofa, curled into a ball. Yet even in sleep, nightmares haunted her. She was standing over Johnny's grave, and he was yelling at her, trying to pull her inside with him. Warning her to stay away from Flint. Reminding her that he had stolen their home, that he hadn't needed her father's land, and that the Double W had been absorbed into the Diamondback. That when Flint found the person trying to sabotage him, his life would return to normal.

But that was impossible for her.

Flint waited until the fire had been completely extinguished and the horses had been located and settled in another barn, then examined by the intern vets before leaving the smoky rubble.

Erring on the side of caution, he assigned two ranch hands to watch the dead embers in case the wind picked up and the fire started up again. The detective had called in two more locals to question his hands. Knowing he couldn't clean up the sight until after the CSI team finished processing it, he stared at the charred remains of the stable for a minute, then climbed in his truck and drove to his house.

Worn out both mentally and physically, he let himself inside, then strode up the stairs for a shower. Once he'd scrubbed and put on fresh clothes, he decided to check on Lora Leigh. God, she'd been courageous and selfless to race into his stable to save his animals.

Especially knowing that the brother she'd buried today might have died because of him.

But when he peeked inside her room, the bed was empty and unmade. Had she finally gotten scared and left the ranch?

Or could something have happened to her?

Fear heated his veins, and he hurried down the steps. Lucinda was already in bed, so he checked the kitchen. Empty.

A noise startled him, and he pivoted, then headed toward the sound. A low moan. Soft and low like a woman's.

He tensed and paused to listen, then realized it was coming from his den. He forced himself to tread quietly as he approached, then leaned inside the doorway. A sliver of moonlight slashed the wall and fell across the sofa, illuminating a figure.

Lora Leigh was stretched out on his sofa.

She looked so at home with her hair spilling over her shoulders, that he imagined picking her up and carrying her to bed—to their bed—where they'd make love until morning.

She moaned softly, and he inched forward, then

leaned over and slid his arms beneath her. Her eyes flickered open slightly, and she looked dazed and confused. "Shh, go back to sleep. I'm taking you up to bed now," he whispered.

She nestled against him, and his body hardened with desire and a fierce protectiveness, which made him hold her tighter. She was so sweet and vulnerable, so strong and tender, so brave and intelligent. And in spite of her mixed feelings for him, she'd put her life on the line for him and his ranch.

A war raged in his head as he carried her up the stairs. He wanted desperately to give something back to her. To let her know that she wasn't alone.

But she'd been through hell today. He couldn't take advantage of her.

His muscles strained as he kept his libido in check. Yet as he gently laid her on the bed, she reached for him. "Flint?"

His throat closed, his lungs fighting for air. Her sultry voice resurrected wicked fantasies that he'd barely allowed himself to think about, much less follow through on.

Like Lora Leigh stripping to give him a glorious view of her bare breasts and distended nipples. Lora Leigh naked and writhing beneath him as he pounded his sex into her.

Lora Leigh with her legs wrapped around his waist— or neck—as he brought her to a mind-shattering orgasm.

Lora Leigh whispering that she loved having him inside her.

"What?" he finally managed to ask in a hoarse voice.

She reached up and threaded her fingers into his hair. "Please don't go."

He dropped his head forward with a pained sigh. "Lora Leigh, you could have died tonight because of me."

"But I didn't," she whispered. "I'm here now and so are you."

Any further protest died on his lips as she drew him down to her and pressed her lips to his.

His pulse pounded as he slid down beside her, pulled her into his arms and ravaged her mouth, hunger and desire burning through him as hot as the fire that had consumed his stable earlier.

Chapter Fifteen

Hunger raged through Flint at lightning speed, but tenderness for Lora Leigh also suffused him, and he pulled back slightly, cupping her face between his hands. "Lora Leigh, I want you. But are you sure?"

Her soft purr as she pulled him closer and traced his jaw with her finger sent a surge of emotion and desire through him. "Yes. Please, Flint…"

He felt humbled and ecstatic at the same time, his body throbbing and pulsing with raw desire.

Then she reached for the shirt that he hadn't bothered to button and ran her hands over his bare chest, and all humbleness fled as pure need coursed through him.

He teased her lips apart with his tongue and threaded his fingers into her hair, savoring the silky strands as he inhaled her fresh, soapy scent. Lora Leigh wasn't perfume and prissiness, like some of the society women who hounded him for his money.

She was tough and strong and sexy and…real.

She deepened the kiss, her tongue dancing with his, and

he wedged his leg between hers, drinking in her essence and showing her just how much he wanted her with his own frenzied kiss. Lips met lips, hands began to roam and tease, and he groaned when her tongue traced his nipple and moved across the wide expanse of his chest.

His sex throbbed; his heart hammered; his whole body felt as if it would combust in seconds.

He had to slow things down.

Pushing her hands away from him, he lifted them above her head and gripped her wrists, forcing her to stop her torture so he could taste her all over. She moaned, her body rubbing against his like a cat in heat, and he caught her moan with his mouth, then tugged her camisole up with his teeth so he could lick a trail down her neck and breasts. Perspiration tickled his neck as he finally pulled one taut nipple between his lips and suckled her.

A raging need shot through him, and she parted her legs in invitation, welcoming his hard body between her thighs. He laved her breasts, gently restraining her so she could feel every delicious tongue thrash as he licked his way down to her navel.

He wanted her naked. Wanted to feel and touch every inch of her flesh.

His body pulsing with need, he released her hands to tear off her tap pants. She jammed her hands into his hair, with a moan, as he slid his hands beneath her hips and lifted her for a sampling.

"Flint…"

"Ride it out, baby," he whispered. "I've been wanting to do this ever since I laid eyes on you."

A soft sigh of pleasure escaped her as her own breath puffed out, and she held on to him as he sipped at her inner thighs, then feathered kisses over the core of her desire.

He teased the nub into his mouth and threw her legs over his shoulders, his sex aching as her body quivered around him.

Her sweet taste filled him, made him feel a tightness in his chest, and even before she reached her peak, he craved the taste of her again.

She whimpered his name and reached for him, and pleasure rocketed through him so intensely for a moment that he thought he might climax himself.

She tugged at his jeans, and he hastily jerked them off, along with his boxers. Then she reached for him. Her hand closed around his length, and she began to stroke him in a sultry way, sending fire shouting through his loins.

"Lora Leigh, baby, I need to be inside you."

She traced a thumb over the tip of his erection and reached for a condom. Together they rolled it on, and she opened her legs wider. Then he guided his engorged head to her tip to tease her moist center before he filled her. She gripped his hips, digging her heels into his backside as he thrust inside her, then began to hammer into her.

He wanted to go slow, ordered himself to think of her pleasure, but her throaty sounds and pleas sent him into a frenzy of lust, and he angled her hips upward, thrusting so deeply inside her that pure, exquisite ecstasy coursed through him in waves.

His own guttural groan seemed to trigger a second orgasm for her, and they clung together, bodies pounding and joining, breathing erratic, his heart melding with hers as they plummeted over the crest together.

TREMORS ROCKED THROUGH Lora Leigh, triggering a torrent of erotic sensations, which spiraled through every nerve ending in her body. She clung to Flint, knowing she'd never felt this way with a man before, and that she might never again.

His breath bathed her neck as he collapsed on top of her, and even though he'd climaxed, he still held her tightly, his big shoulders shuddering against hers, his hair tickling her neck. She buried her face in the sultry smell of his masculine body and closed her eyes, willing the moment to last forever and erase the pain and grief tormenting her.

But even as she tried to forget reality, it crashed down on her, and moisture pooled in her eyes.

He lifted his head and looked at her, his expression troubled. "I didn't want to make you cry," he said gruffly.

"It's not you," she said, although in truth, her feelings for him confused her even more. "It's just been an emotional day."

"I know." He gently pushed her hair from her face and kissed her forehead. "Do you still want me to stay?"

The insecurity in his deep voice sent an overwhelming sense of desire and need through her again. "Yes," she whispered. "I don't want to be alone."

He lowered his head and pressed his lips to hers in the sweetest, most tantalizing kiss of her life. Then he rolled off her, went to the bathroom and disposed of the condom, returned and cradled her in his arms.

"You're not alone," he whispered hoarsely. "Go to sleep, Lora Leigh. I'll be here in the morning. And in the night, to chase away your nightmares."

His touch, his words, the scent of him and the feel of his legs as they brushed against hers soothed her, and she closed her eyes and melted against him. For just tonight, she'd stay with Flint.

Then tomorrow… She didn't want to contemplate the reality daylight would bring. She wanted to savor the moment and pretend that she had a chance with Flint.

When she awoke a few hours later, with sunlight streaming through the sheers and Flint spooning her, his thick shaft wedged between her buttocks, her body came alive, heady with hunger and a warm dampness already pooling between her thighs.

Yearning to taste him the way he had her, she pressed a kiss to his chest, then dropped tender, hungry kisses down his chest and stomach until she reached his jutting, hard erection. Craving closeness, she teased his tip with her tongue, then closed her lips around his engorged head and drew him into her mouth.

He moaned, and she felt his hands slide down to drag her upward, but she grabbed them and pushed them to his sides, restraining him so she could do as she pleased.

She wanted him desperately.

She tasted and licked him, smiling at the tortured sound of his voice as he called her name. "Lora Leigh, stop…."

With a guttural groan, he jerked her away, then flipped her to her back and climbed above her, his eyes hooded with arousal. "Come here, baby. I want you," he said on a ragged breath.

She smiled in invitation and opened for him, her climax teetering on the edge at the first nudge of his length inching inside her. He was so big, she swallowed back a moan and arched her back to accommodate his fullness. He claimed her mouth with his and thrust inside her, all the way to her core. She whimpered, clutched his hips and held on for the ride of her life as he pumped furiously in and out of her, deepening the movements until her body trembled with pleasure exploding through her.

He came with a groan, their bodies quivering together. Then he rolled to the side and took her with him, kissing her lips and neck as the aftermath of their lovemaking rocked through them. Smiling with contentment, she closed her eyes and fell back asleep, then dreamed that nothing could keep them apart, that they would be together this way forever.

But an hour later she awakened and found the bed empty. Pushing her tangled hair from her face, she sat up slowly, feeling lost and bereft without Flint beside her.

Then she spotted her father's suicide letter on her dresser, and she dropped her head into her hands.

God help her. She had fallen hopelessly in love with Flint.

And in doing so, she'd betrayed her family.

FLINT WANTED NOTHING MORE than to go back to bed with Lora Leigh. But daylight and a call from Detective Green had brought him back to reality and the fact that he might have lost Lora Leigh the night before in that fire.

And after making love to her, he couldn't lose her.

"Look, McKade, Howard Reed and McElroy both have alibis for last night, and you said yourself that Tate wasn't there. I think you have to face the fact that your trouble may be due to an inside job."

Flint scrubbed a hand over his beard stubble.

"This has to be someone you trust," Detective Green continued, "someone working for you who has easy access to your land, to your plans and schedule."

Flint sighed. As much as he hated to admit it or distrust his employees, his gut told him that Detective Green might be right. That one of them was working against him.

"I'll look over the list personally," Flint said, thinking he'd have to try to pinpoint a worker he'd pissed off recently.

"I'll look at their financial records," Detective Green suggested. "If one of your employees had financial problems, he might have taken a payoff to help sabotage you."

"Hell, Green, half of my employees probably have financial problems. In case you haven't noticed, the economy is tight right now."

"True, but it's a possibility. Have you heard from Jabar?"

Flint frowned and paced the hallway. "No. Akeem said he's in Turkey."

"Well, one thing is for sure. This guy is escalating. First, the attack at the airport, then on Lora Leigh and now your stable. Sounds like he's not going to stop until he destroys you or is caught."

Flint glanced at Lora Leigh's closed door. He'd thought that having her close would enable him to protect her. But what if keeping her near him put her in more danger?

"Anyway, the crime scene unit is on its way."

"Thanks," Flint said, distracted by worry for Lora Leigh. "I've had men watching the stable all night to secure it. I'll meet them at the stable."

He disconnected the call, then made a snap decision. Too many deaths lay at his feet now, haunting him. An image of Lora Leigh lying on the floor of the burning stable sent a fresh wave of terror though his nerve endings.

Sweat exploded on his skin. He couldn't stand it if anything happened to her.

He had to make her leave the ranch. He had to get her out of his life. It was the only way to protect her.

Inhaling deeply to calm the anxiety clawing at his insides, he knocked gently on the door, then went inside. Lora Leigh had just stepped from the bathroom. Her hair dangled in wet ringlets around her shoulders, and she hugged the cotton robe to her, but her nipples strained the thin fabric. A blush stained her cheeks, and desire simmered in her beautiful eyes.

His own body hardened in response, the need to have her again gripping him with an intensity that threatened to make him change his mind about sending her away.

But keeping her here was selfish and was endangering her life.

"Flint?"

"Pack your things, Lora Leigh. I want you to leave the ranch."

Her eyes widened in confusion. "What? Why?"

He hesitated; he knew how stubborn she could be,

that if he told her he was trying to protect her, she'd argue and insist on staying.

Because she wanted to clear her brother's name.

He wanted that for her sake, but he had to know the truth. And her father's secret still stood between them like an albatross around his neck.

He gestured toward the bed and then waved his hand between them. "This is just not going to work. We both know that. After all, you've been lining up your replacement for days."

Anger and suspicion darkened her eyes, and she grabbed his arm. "I heard you on the phone. Was it about Johnny?"

His mouth thinned. "No. But the CSI team is on the way, and Detective Green is questioning my employees to see if one of them is working against me. Besides, it's not safe here right now, and I'd rather not complicate things with—" he gestured toward the bed "—a personal relationship."

"But the horses—"

"I have other vets," he said curtly. "And don't worry about your salary. You'll be compensated with a nice severance package."

"I don't want your damn money."

"Don't be foolish, Lora Leigh. You earned it."

Her face contorted with emotions—anger, hurt… shame.

God, he was making a mess of this. But if she knew he'd lied about her father, that revealing that lie might have saved her brother, she'd hate him even more.

At least this way she'd be safe.

"So that's it? You finally got me in bed and now you're throwing me out?"

Furious, she snatched her suitcase and started tossing clothes inside. This time he didn't stop her or argue.

He left the room so she could pack.

But his heart ached as he walked down the steps to his office. He'd done the right thing by pushing her away.

But he hadn't expected it to hurt so damn much.

LORA LEIGH HAULED HER suitcase down the stairs, and Lucinda met her at the door.

"You are leaving us?" Lucinda asked, with an odd expression in her eyes.

"Yes," Lora Leigh said. "At Mr. McKade's request."

Lucinda's eyes widened in surprise. "I don't understand, *señorita.*"

"I guess he no longer needs my services." She offered a forced smile. "Thank you for everything you've done to make me feel at home here, Lucinda."

"*Sí.*"

Lora Leigh's chest was aching from struggling to hold back tears. She'd been such a fool to think that Flint cared for her. That they had a chance for a future.

Swallowing back tears, she secured her computer bag over her shoulder, carried her overnight bag to the car. She made a quick stop at the cottage to retrieve the rest of her things, then drove toward the horse barns. She had to check on the Arabians before she left. Dammit, she cared about them, too.

She stopped at the quarantine barn, went in and checked Eastern Promise and Iron Legs. Both looked more alert, and their eyes clearer. She petted each one in turn, glad to see they had more energy and their symptoms were subsiding, then headed to the other barn to check on Sir Huon and Lord Myers.

But her cell phone rang as she entered, and she checked the number. The lab.

Maybe they finally had the test results. If so, at least she could pass on what they were dealing with to Flint's vets, so she connected the call as she settled in the driver's seat. "Dr. Whittaker speaking."

"Lora Leigh, it's Jim Braxton."

"Yes?"

"Sorry it took me so long, but it got crazy around here. Plus, the tests didn't add up, so I ran a couple more just to be certain."

"What are you talking about?" Lora Leigh asked. "What's wrong?"

"It's not what we thought, after all. No equine flu."

"Are you sure?"

His breathing rattled over the line. "Yes, but it is something to be concerned about."

Her fingers tightened around the cell phone. "Jim, don't keep me in suspense. Just tell me what you found."

"The horses were suffering from a very mild form of radiation poisoning. The symptoms mimic equine flu."

"Radiation poisoning?" Her mind raced with questions. "How would they be exposed?"

"I don't know," Jim said. "But McKade needs to find out. And we'll have to report this to Homeland Security and call in a hazmat team to search his stables and the plane the horses were transported in." He hesitated. "Do you think McKade might have been smuggling something dangerous?"

Nerves clutched Lora Leigh's stomach in a vise. "No. Flint doesn't know. I'm sure of it. But I'll inform him of what we found and the ramifications immediately."

"Lora Leigh, didn't you say one of the ranch hands died with similar symptoms?"

A sick feeling came over her. "Yes. Dear God. I'll have Flint check with the M.E. to see what he found on the autopsy."

"Find out who all was exposed," Jim said. "And be careful."

Her hand was shaking as she hung up. The last thing she wanted to do was talk to Flint right now, but she had to warn him to get the proper precautions and treatment in place and alert him that Homeland Security would have to be involved.

She punched his number and waited, but he didn't answer, so she left a message for him to call her right away, then told him she was driving out to the barn where the Arabians had first been housed to take a look around. When she reached the barn, she looked around for signs of trouble, but no one was in sight, so she slipped inside and began to search the barn. The stalls were empty now, except for the hay scattered on the floor. Frowning, she noticed some tack on the wall in the corner; then her gaze was drawn to the blankets that had come in with the Arabians. Curious, she walked over and started to examine them.

But a noise jarred her—footsteps. Then the barn door screeching open. Was it Flint?

Déjà vu struck her, and her skin prickled. She'd been attacked here before.

Had her assailant returned to kill her this time?

HE WATCHED THE DOCTOR from the shadows, cursing his fate that she'd stopped by. The nosy bitch. She was just as much trouble as her brother had been.

Dammit. He'd assumed everyone would be at the house or working on the ranch. So why had Dr. Whittaker returned to the empty barn today?

Because she suspected something? Had she found the merchandise he'd been sent here to retrieve? Did she know what he and Johnny had been up to?

She'd moved closer to the horse blankets. Her eyes narrowed as she flipped one of them over, as if searching for something.

A tremor started in his hand. Maybe the pieces had been sewn inside.

He couldn't let her find them.

His lungs tight, he inched into the barn, clenching the .38 in his hand.

He'd have to kill her. Using one of McKade's guns was genius. Yes, as he'd thought earlier, he could frame McKade for the murder.

Then he'd be out of the way for good.

Chapter Sixteen

Flint's phone had vibrated as he introduced himself to the crime scene unit, but he was so engrossed in studying the charred embers of his stable that he didn't immediately answer. The smell of burned wood and wood shavings filled the air, the peaceful scents and sights of the land destroyed by unnecessary violence.

"There are definite traces of an accelerant. Smells like gasoline, which anyone could have easily purchased," one of the CSIs said. "We also found matches. I'll let you know when we're finished."

"Thanks."

The CSI nodded, then headed back to the cordoned-off area, and Flint checked his messages. He was surprised to see that the phone call had come from Lora Leigh.

Fearing something else had happened, he quickly listened to the message. What the hell? Radiation poisoning? How had that happened?

He had to see Lora Leigh and discuss how to proceed.

He told the CSI to call him with his discoveries, then

hit Redial to call Lora Leigh, but she didn't answer, so he jogged toward his horse.

Anxiety immediately tightened his chest. He'd asked Lora Leigh to leave to protect her, and he didn't like the idea of her being anywhere on his property alone. What if the radiation exposure had occurred on his ranch, even somewhere in that barn, and that was the reason Roy Parkman got sick and died?

He climbed on Fever and headed toward the barn, phoning the ME as he rode. He left a message asking if he'd discovered any evidence of radiation poisoning in Parkman, then galloped past the pasture where some of the mares were roaming. He spotted Lora Leigh's truck in the distance and wondered why she hadn't answered the phone.

Suddenly a gunshot rang out, and his heart stopped, panic zinging through his chest.

The shot had come from the barn.

He gave Fever a firm kick and a command to go, dust flying behind him as he raced to the barn. Tensing as he approached, he slowed Fever, then slid off the stallion and removed the pistol he kept tucked in his jeans in case he came upon a snake.

He eased up to the barn, listening for sounds of a scream or voices, then heard Lora Leigh whimper.

"Why are you doing this?"

He peered inside the barn and saw a man dragging Lora Leigh toward the back doorway, a gun pointed at her head.

His heart hammered with fear.

Light spilled in from the open barn door, and he

saw the man's face. Sylvester Robbins. The man who'd coordinated the transportation of his horses to the auction house.

A man who'd worked for him for five years. A man he'd trusted.

Dammit, he couldn't let him kill Lora Leigh.

LORA LEIGH DUG HER FINGERNAILS into Sylvester Robbins's arm where he'd wrapped it around her neck. "Just tell me why?" she pleaded.

"For the money. Why else?" he growled.

"I don't understand." Lora Leigh's heart raced as she tried to stall. Surely Flint would check his messages and come and find her.

Unless he didn't want to see her...

"You'd hurt these horses for money?" she whispered.

"It's more than that," Robbins snarled. "I had to. My daughter was ill. She would have died without surgery."

"Was my brother working for you?" Lora Leigh asked.

Robbins spit a wad of chewing tobacco on the barn floor. "Yeah, at first. Then he backed out at the last minute and tried to call it off."

"And that got him killed?" Lora Leigh murmured.

"You're damn right, just like your nosiness is going to get you killed." Robbins's fingers dug into her back as he pressed the barrel of the gun to her temple.

"Stop it, Robbins," Flint shouted.

Lora Leigh jerked her gaze toward the front where Flint stood, a mass of fury radiating from him, his gun pointed at Robbins. "Let her go, Robbins. If you have a bone to pick, it's with me. Not her."

Robbins cursed. "It's too late. She knows too much."

"She doesn't know anything," Flint said. "She's just a vet that I fired a little while ago. Now tell me who you're working for."

"Why do you think I'm working for someone?" Robbins asked. "Don't you think I could pull this off myself?"

"No," Flint said in a lethal tone. "You're getting paid. I heard you tell Lora Leigh."

Lora Leigh flinched, but Flint's gaze met hers, and emotions flashed in his eyes that shocked her. Did he actually care about her? Even after he'd told her to leave?

"Listen to me," Flint said, walking slowly toward them. "I'll give you whatever you want. Money. A deal to get away. Just let her go, and we'll work out something."

"No," Robbins snapped. "You have everything and I have nothing."

Flint's brows arched in confusion, and Lora Leigh sucked in a sharp breath, dizzy with fear. But if she was going to die, she wanted Flint to know what Robbins had been up to. The reasons his ranch hands and pilot had died, and his Arabians had suffered. "When the lab called about radiation poisoning, I thought something in the barn might have made them sick. So I came here to look around."

Robbins gripped her neck and she coughed, gasping for air. "You found them, didn't you?"

She nodded, and again, Flint frowned. But he'd been slowly creeping toward them and now was only a few feet away. "What's going on, Lora Leigh?"

"They're smuggling something inside the horse

blankets," she whispered hoarsely. "Some kind of small parts. It might be materials to make a bomb."

Shock registered on Flint's face. "A bomb? My God, Robbins, what are you up to?"

"I CAN'T TELL YOU." ROBBINS dragged Lora Leigh back another step, and Flint's pulse galloped. He couldn't let her die.

Slowly, he inched a foot forward, but Robbins cocked the gun, and Lora Leigh's eyes widened. Their gazes locked, his full of regret and promises, hers full of what he wanted to think was forgiveness and…love.

A second later, determination darkened her eyes, and she suddenly stomped on Robbins's foot, raised her elbow and jammed it in his side. He yelped in shock and dropped his grip for a moment; then she dived down to the floor and rolled toward an open stall. Flint fired a shot, but Robbins dodged sideways and fired.

Flint's body bounced backward, pain splintering his shoulder as the bullet pierced skin and muscle. Blood spurted from his arm, his legs gave way and he sank to the floor. He lost precious seconds, and his gun slid across the barn floor.

He tried to get up, but a dizzy spell assaulted him, and he swayed and fell backward again, losing his balance.

With a roar of pure fear, Robbins scrambled after Lora Leigh.

She screamed and Flint blinked to see what was happening. Robbins caught her, and they rolled across the floor, limbs tangling. She struggled to escape, managed to get to her hands and knees, and kicked wildly at him, but he grabbed her ankle and dragged her toward him. She fell face forward, clawing at the floor for control, but Robbins was relentless and reached for her other ankle. She swung her foot up and connected with his chin, and he bellowed, then lunged after her again, determined to subdue her.

Flint blinked to focus and dragged himself up, searching frantically for his gun, but he didn't see it anywhere. Dammit. He didn't have time to search.

"Flint!"

Robbins caught her and slammed his fist into her face. She fell backward with a moan and pure hatred swelled in Flint, obliterating any thought of calling the cops. He'd end this himself.

Bolstered by adrenaline and rage, Flint spotted the pitchfork in the corner, latched on to it, then staggered upright and vaulted forward. The pitchfork landed in the center of Robbins's back.

He howled in agony as the prongs sank into his flesh, hands flailing for control but failing as blood spewed from his back. Lora Leigh screamed as his weight collapsed on top of her, her hands battling to push him off her.

Pain shot through Flint's shoulder and chest, ripping him in two, but he forced his feet forward and yanked Robbins off Lora Leigh, then rolled him to his side. His eyes were stark wide with terror and pain, his mouth gaping open, the last breath heaving from his chest in a torrent of anger.

"Not over..."

Then his head lolled to the side, and his body jerked and went slack.

Lora Leigh covered her face with her hands, and Flint staggered to her, knelt and pulled her into his arms. She fell against him with a sob, and he kissed her hair, grateful she was alive.

LORA LEIGH HAD NEVER BEEN so terrified in her life, both for herself and for Flint.

She lifted her head and saw blood soaking his shirt, so she pulled away. "I'm calling for help."

He leaned against the stall railing and nodded, his complexion paling. She ran and grabbed a towel from the washroom, then returned and pressed it to his wound. "Keep pressure on it."

Then she frantically reached for her cell phone. Dr. Hardin answered on the third ring, and she explained the circumstances.

"I'll call an ambulance and be right there," Dr. Hardin assured her.

"Thanks," Lora Leigh replied.

"Call Detective Green," Flint said, with a wince. "We need to report this."

She nodded, willing him to hang on until the doctor arrived; then she punched in the detective's number.

"Detective Green speaking."

"It's Lora Leigh Whittaker. You need to come out to the Diamondback. There's been a shooting. One of Flint's employees is dead, and Flint has been shot." She wiped at the grime on her face, which she'd obtained when rolling on the barn floor with Robbins.

"I'm on my way."

Detective Green hung up, and she heard a car pull up,

so she raced outside to meet the doctor. The ambulance's siren cut into the tense silence, and she waved Dr. Hardin in to treat Flint.

The next twenty minutes passed in a chaotic blur as the paramedics loaded Flint into the ambulance and the detective arrived. Flint was weak and starting to fade, but he refused to leave until he spoke to the detective.

"I think Robbins was working for someone else," Flint said through gritted teeth. "But he didn't say who. He was here looking for the bomb parts he'd smuggled in inside the horse blankets."

Detective Green cleared his throat. "So that was what the attack was all about at the airport. They were probably trying to sneak the merchandise out at the airport so you wouldn't know what they were doing, but your men caught them, and all hell broke loose. So he came here looking for the horse blankets before."

"Yeah, and Lora Leigh was in the barn," Flint said, "so he assaulted her."

"Then the horses got sick from the radiation, although the quantity they were exposed to wasn't lethal, because of their size," Lora Leigh said.

Flint grimaced. "Unfortunately, Roy Parkman wasn't so lucky."

Lora Leigh nodded. "We have to alert Homeland Security so they can investigate. They'll want a hazmat team to come in, measure the level of radiation, and possibly put decontamination procedures into place."

"I'll take care of that," Detective Green said.

Flint massaged his shoulder, swaying again, feeling

weak. "This won't be completely over until we find out who Robbins was working for."

Lora Leigh nodded, wanting to say more, to apologize for her brother, but Flint needed to get to the hospital.

Dr. Hardin waved a hand. "It's time to go, Flint. You've lost a good bit of blood."

Flint nodded, his eyes glazing over, and the paramedics closed the door to the ambulance and sped away.

She stared out across the Diamondback, a well of sadness engulfing her.

She'd come here to get revenge and to find her brother, but she'd fallen in love with the man she'd seen as her enemy. But a life with Flint was impossible.

It was time to leave. This ranch wasn't home to her and never would be. Not after all that had happened.

Chapter Seventeen

One week later

Flint rubbed at his shoulder as he descended the stairs, grateful to finally shed the sling.

He was still sore, but the pain in his shoulder was nothing compared to the empty, hollow burning inside his chest.

For the past few years, he'd thought all he needed was his business, his empire and the Aggie Four to be complete, that and an occasional roll in the hay with a sexy, available woman.

No commitments involved. No romantic entanglements to sidetrack him.

But that was before Lora Leigh had swept into his life and knocked him off his feet.

Her love of her family, devotion to his horses, and courage were a refreshing change from the money-hungry, social-climbing women who'd offered themselves to him as if they were steak on a platter.

"Señor McKade," Lucinda said. "Señor Willis

from Homeland Security is waiting for you in your office."

"Thank you, Lucinda." The past week had been hell, dealing with them and the hazmat team. Lora Leigh and her friend Dr. Braxton had prescribed treatment for the horses, coordinating with Flint's other staff vets, and the horses were making a remarkable recovery.

With the removal of the bomb parts and decontamination, his ranch was almost back to normal. Still, he'd hired extra security to watch his property for a few days to make sure the danger was over and that the bomb hadn't been meant for him.

He pushed open the door and shook hands with Willis. "Any progress on the investigation?"

"We still haven't located Jabar, but Mr. Abdul received a text message saying Jabar would be back in the States to discuss the problem shortly. He denies any knowledge of the bomb parts."

Flint rolled his shoulder in an attempt to relieve the throbbing.

Willis continued, "And your friend Mr. Abdul agreed to look into his associates and employees at the auction house. If the bomb wasn't meant for you, we've got bigger problems and need to figure out the target."

Flint nodded. "Yes, we discussed that."

Willis stood. "We'll be in touch if we find out who Robbins was working for. We appreciate your cooperation, Mr. McKade."

"I want to get to the bottom of this as much as you do. I don't like being used. The men who died because of this deserve justice."

"And we don't like the idea of a new terrorist cell cropping up." Willis turned and left, leaving Flint alone and frustrated. He sensed the danger to him was over. But he still wanted to know the answer to the larger picture.

He also wanted Lora Leigh back, dammit.

But she must still blame him for her father's death. And now for Johnny's.

Would it make a difference if she knew the truth, or would she still hate him?

He shifted, rubbing at his shoulder. He wished to God he'd never made that deal with Whittaker.

That was one deal he could undo. After all, he didn't want or need the land, and Lora Leigh deserved to have her home.

He opened his files, located the deed to the Double W, then called his lawyer. A half hour later, he met him in town, signed the deed over to Lora Leigh, then had it couriered to the room she was renting in town.

If he couldn't have her, he'd at least feel better knowing she had her ranch to go home to.

DUSK HAD FALLEN, THE LAST strains of sunlight reminding Lora Leigh that another day had passed. Another day alone.

She had rented a room in town until she could decide where she wanted to move. She couldn't imagine living anywhere but Texas, but even with the state as big as it was, it seemed too close to Flint and the Diamondback.

When she closed her eyes, memories smothered her. She could still smell the scent of fresh grass and hay;

hear Flint's horses galloping across the pasture; see him riding up on a stallion with that black Stetson shading his eyes; hear his deep, rumbling, sexy voice calling her name in the heat of passion.

She could feel his big hands on her, his lips and mouth and fingers teasing her, bringing her to ecstasy.

Trying to shake away the taunting memories, she went to her file box and removed her father's letter and reread it.

He'd told her to follow her dreams. His had been of the ranch. Hers had been to become a vet.

But she wanted more in her life. A family of her own. A man to love her and share her life with. She wanted Flint.

Impossible.

The doorbell rang, and she hurried to the door, half hoping it was Flint, but a courier stood on the doorstep. "I have a package for Dr. Whittaker."

She accepted the envelope, signed for it, then closed the door and read the return signature. Flint McKade.

Probably paperwork related to her severance package.

She almost tossed it aside but decided to get it over with, so she opened the envelope. Shock filled her. It was the deed to her father's ranch.

Flint had signed it over to her.

But why?

Did he feel sorry for her? Feel as if he owed her because of her father's death and Johnny's death? Because he'd hired her, then dismissed her after they made love?

It didn't make sense. She certainly didn't want his charity or pity.

And as much as she wanted to blame him for

Johnny's death, she realized now that Johnny's quest for vengeance had led him to his own murder.

All the more reason she didn't want to live with hate inside her. She had to forgive Flint, her father and brother for leaving her.

But she couldn't go back to the Double W and live so close to Flint....

She scrambled through her father's papers to find the documents outlining his original deal with Flint, but an envelope from the hospital caught her eye.

She frowned and removed a piece of paper from the envelope and discovered it was a medical report, complete with pathology results.

Her hands trembled as she read it. Her father had been diagnosed with an inoperable brain tumor.

She swayed and clawed at the desk, dizzy with confusion and shock. When had he found out?

Her eyes shot to the date, and grief swelled in her throat. Three weeks before her father had committed suicide. Three weeks before he'd sold the ranch to Flint.

She collapsed into the chair, questions flooding her. Why hadn't her father told her he was ill? Why had he sold the ranch, instead of leaving it to her and Johnny?

Frantic for answers, she retrieved her cell phone and called Dr. Murdock. His answering machine picked up, and she left a message to call her immediately.

Nerves knotted her stomach, and she paced the room, searching for answers. She felt as if she'd lost her father all over again, as if he'd betrayed her by not confiding the truth. They could have had more tests done. He could have undergone chemo and radiation, consulted specialists…

Tears rolled down her cheeks, and she gulped back a sob.

She glanced at the deed again and knew what she had to do. Hands shaking, she crammed the deed back into the envelope, then slid it inside her bag and headed to the door to take it back to Flint. She might not have anything left, but she had her reputation and her pride, and she'd damn well not lose them.

Her phone rang as soon as she got in the truck. Dr. Murdock. She quickly connected the call.

"Hi, Lora Leigh. What can I do for you?"

"Is it true that my father had a brain tumor?"

Dead silence met her question.

"Is it?" she repeated.

He cleared his throat. "Yes. You didn't know?"

"No," she said, tears lacing her voice. "Why didn't he tell me?"

He sighed. "I advised him to tell both you and Johnny, but you know your father. He was a stubborn, proud man. He didn't want to be sick or a burden."

"He wouldn't have been a burden," Lora Leigh cried. "We would have taken care of him, taken him to a specialist. He could have had treatment." Her voice cracked. "He didn't have to die."

Another tense silence. "I'm sorry, Lora Leigh. But he was dying, and the treatment would have prolonged his life only a couple of months. He didn't want to go like that." He hesitated, then continued. "And you know your father. He was practical and didn't want what little money he had to go to medical care and you and Johnny to be left with nothing."

"But didn't he understand that we didn't care about the money? We loved him."

"I know," Dr. Murdock said. "And he knew that, too. But in the end, he chose what he wanted to do, and none of us could have stopped him."

Lora Leigh was crying openly now, grief and anger gripping her chest. Maybe the best thing she could do was to leave Texas.

She didn't want the Double W now. There were too many sad memories and ghosts on the property.

Flint had bought it, and she'd give it back to him, then pack her things and get as far away from her father's land and the Diamondback as she could.

Then she could start over and forget she'd ever known Flint McKade.

FLINT SADDLED FEVER AND rode out to check the Arabians, then his broodmares. Hopefully, Lora Leigh had received his gift by now, and maybe she would be able to go home, instead of living in that two-bit rental place she'd moved into. Knowing she was there tormented him.

The need to feel the late-night air on his face made him nudge Fever toward the Double W property. He used to sleep like a baby in his house, but now memories of Lora Leigh tortured him. Her ponytail swishing as she jogged down the steps at dawn for coffee in those tight jeans. Her intoxicating fragrance lingered in the guest suite, on the pillows and in the air.

And the feel of her hands on him, her lips kissing his, moving over his hard length, her body welcoming him inside, taunted him every time he closed his damn eyes.

He understood more than anyone the draw of the land, the craving for fresh air, the need to touch the dirt with your fingers and own a piece of heaven that you called home.

Just as Lora Leigh and her father had.

He studied the small white clapboard house where she'd grown up, the porch swing, the bird feeders her mother had in the yard, and hoped she could be happy here again.

Suddenly, the pounding of horse hooves sounded behind him, and he jerked his head around and saw Lora Leigh riding toward him, her long hair flowing in the breeze. He was so starved for her, so thirsty for another taste of her, that for a moment, he thought he was seeing a mirage.

But she slapped the reins against Sly's side, urging him to speed up, and he knew she was real. Dust spewed behind her, and his heart beat faster as she approached. She wore a thin tank top and jeans but no hat this time, and as she neared, he noticed that her eyes were red and puffy.

His gut tightened. He'd hoped that she was finally healing, that getting her land back might put a smile on her face and ease her suffering.

Instead of a smile, though, she looked furious.

She pulled on the reins, slowing Sly to a halt in front of him, but not before he saw her glance at her childhood home with a tortured look. Then she jerked an envelope from the saddlebag and shoved it at him. "What in the hell is this?"

He narrowed his eyes as he opened it. "The deed to the Double W."

"Why did you send it to me?"

He frowned, confused by her angry tone. Then he said the only thing he could—the truth. "Because it belongs to you. And it's standing between us."

Shock showed in her deep blue eyes. "You bought it fair and square, Flint. I don't want your pity or charity."

She spun around from him to ride away, but he grabbed her arm. "I didn't give it to you because I pitied you. I gave it to you because I know how much you love it."

Her lower lip quivered. "Not anymore," she whispered.

"I don't believe that," Flint said. He climbed down from his horse, then pulled her down beside him, gripped her arms and turned her to face her parents' house. "This was your home, and you loved it just like your father did."

"If my father loved it so damn much, why did he sell it to you? Why didn't he stick around so he could keep it?"

He cleared his throat, aching to tell her the truth, to pull her into his arms, but he'd given her father his word. And he didn't want to hurt her any more than she had already been hurt. "Sometimes we do things that don't make sense to others," he said gruffly. "But with good reason."

Her eyes raked over him, with suspicion. "What?"

He gritted his teeth.

"You knew, didn't you?" Anger sharpened her words. "You knew that he was sick. And you bought the property and took advantage of him, just like I thought in the beginning."

He shook his head, and she suddenly balled her hands into fists and slammed them into his chest. "You did, didn't you?"

Dammit. He couldn't stand for her to hate him. Not when he loved her so much, he could hardly breathe. "No, Lora Leigh, that's not the way it happened," he said in a hoarse voice.

She pounded at his chest. "Yes, it is. You knew and didn't tell me. Why didn't someone tell me?" She dropped her head forward, with a heart-wrenching sob, utterly defeated. "Why did I have to find out from a medical report after he was gone and it was too late?"

Tears spilled over her lashes, soaking his shirt, and he wrapped his arms around her. "Because your father made me promise not to tell you. That was part of the deal."

She suddenly stilled, her expression a mixture of hurt and agony as she looked up at him.

Flint stroked her arms, lowering his voice. "Your father came to me and asked me if I'd buy his land," he said. "He told me he was ill, dying, and that he didn't want to use all his money for medical care and leave you and your brother with nothing."

"But he loved that land more than anything," Lora Leigh whispered.

Flint cupped her face in his hands and pushed her damp hair from her cheeks. "No, Lora Leigh. He loved the land, but he loved *you* more." His chest squeezed. "Just like I do. That's the reason I returned the deed to you."

"What?"

"I don't want the land," Flint said, with his heart in his throat. "I never did. But I do want you, Lora Leigh. I love you, and if you can forgive me and let me in your life, I promise I'll do everything I can to make you happy."

"Oh, Flint…"

Her voice quivered, and more tears pooled in her eyes. He brushed them away, his heart breaking.

A tense moment of silence stretched between them; then, miraculously, a slow smile lit her eyes. "I love you, too."

His throat closed. "You do?"

"Yes…I didn't want to, but I do." She swallowed, then stood on tiptoe and kissed him. He drank in her taste, so starved for her he thought he might strip her and take her right there on the land, in front of God and the world.

But reality forced him to slow himself, and he searched her face. "Did you mean it?"

"Yes." The sun slid into the horizon, streaking the sky with purple and orange; a cacophony of birds twittered and fluttered down around the bird feeders; and behind them, the sound of his cattle echoed across the land.

"And I love the Diamondback, too," she whispered.

He dropped to his knees on the line dividing the two properties, then took her hand in his. "Then you'll marry me?"

She pressed her hand to her mouth, emotions glittering in her eyes. "Yes."

He stood and swooped her into his arms and kissed her with all the pent-up passion and love he possessed. Lora Leigh and he would marry and join their lives and property.

And they would live happily ever after.

Epilogue

Three months later

Flint could hardly believe his wedding day had arrived. He dressed in his custom-designed western tux with his long black duster coat and platinum boot tips—Lora Leigh's choice—and headed down the steps. Outside, white linen tables had been set up on the lawn, and the gazebo by the pond had been decorated with red roses and lilies for the ceremony. Music from the harpist and piano player filled the balmy air as the guests arrived and were seated.

The past month had been frenetic. Homeland Security had finally cleared him of suspicion, but Jabar was still missing. The Arabians were healthy; his ranch was free of any evidence that radioactive parts had been present. And thankfully, the danger and sabotage against him had ceased.

Taylor and Christopher had also moved to the ranch temporarily until she could get on her feet, and she and Lora Leigh had become fast friends.

Akeem and Jackson were waiting on him at the foot of the stairs, both of them grinning.

"I never thought I'd see this day," Jackson said.

Flint laughed. "Me neither."

Akeem looked slightly sheepish. "I hope you don't mind, but I brought a friend today, Flint. She needs a job and is great with horses and could work as a groom."

Flint smiled, although his curiosity was piqued. At one time he'd thought that his sister and Akeem might have had a thing for each other, but maybe he'd been wrong.

"Sure. I can always use help."

He exited the side door, then climbed on Diamond Daddy and guided him toward the gazebo. Cameras flashed, and murmurs rippled through the crowd. Guests filled the white chairs, the wedding having morphed into a big, blow-out affair. Although they'd discussed keeping the ceremony intimate, he'd wanted everyone in Texas to know he was taking a bride. And, of course, his employees and all their Aggie friends had to attend.

For a moment, a pang of sadness squeezed his chest, the absence of Lora Leigh's family and Viktor threatening to dampen his mood.

But somehow he knew they were watching from heaven and would be pleased for the two of them. He'd also insisted she make his house her own by redecorating their bedroom and den. She'd brought the quilt her mother had made for her—a wedding ring quilt—for their marriage bed.

Diamond Daddy stopped in front of the gazebo, and he angled the horse so he could watch his bride ride up. The last strains of the sun had faded to a red and purple as her angelic form appeared. She was riding her own horse, Miss Sassy, a palomino she'd had at the Double W, symbolic of them joining their lives and ranches.

The long white vintage dress she wore swirled around her ankles as she approached, a single red rose in her hair, which she wore in some kind of knot of curls at the nape of her neck.

He couldn't wait to remove those pins and sink his hands into her long tresses tonight. She slowed her horse to a walk, her gaze meeting his as the wedding march began. And when she joined him and placed her hand in his, his heart swelled with love and pride.

LORA LEIGH'S HEART FLUTTERED with love as Flint danced her across the dance floor, the wedding ceremony and reception a hazy blur of faces, cameras and smiles.

She'd made peace with her family and their choices, although today she missed them most of all. Flint had suggested that her father had known what he was doing when he sold the ranch to Flint, that maybe he'd thought it would bring the two of them together. She didn't know if that was true, but it was a romantic thought.

"I love you, Lora Leigh," Flint whispered as they finished their last dance of the night and hurried toward the limousine. They were taking Flint's private jet to the French Riviera for their honeymoon. Flint had told her he wanted to show her the world, and she'd told him she already had the world in his arms.

Instead of driving straight to the airport, though, Flint asked the driver to stop by her old home.

"What are we doing?" Lora Leigh asked.

The driver parked and Flint gestured toward the bird feeders in the yard, the ones her mother had loved so much.

"I wanted to give you your wedding gift."

Lora Leigh glanced at him in confusion and gestured toward the enormous platinum-setting diamond engagement ring he'd bought her and the band of glittering diamonds he'd given her today. "What else could you give me?"

He kissed her tenderly, then gestured toward the Double W land. "In honor of your mother and father, who loved the land so much, I thought we might turn your property into a bird sanctuary and wildlife preserve."

Tears filled Lora Leigh's eyes. "Oh, Flint, that's a wonderful idea. My parents would be delighted."

He smiled, his eyes skating hungrily over her. She'd never known she could love anyone as much as she did him.

He took her hand in his and kissed it tenderly. "I only wish I could give you back your family."

Lora Leigh's heart clenched. "We both know you can't, just as I can't give you back your best friend or the men you lost."

He pulled her into his arms, and they held each other for a long time, each haunted by the unnecessary loss created by anger, false truths and the need for revenge.

He kissed her tenderly, then pulled back and cupped her face in his hands. "We could make our own family."

"Oh, Flint," she said softly, then placed her hand on

his jaw. "I want children. And I'd like to name our first son after my father."

"Of course."

She smiled and glanced at her old home. "Your gift is so special. But I don't have a gift for you."

His eyes twinkled, and he traced a finger over her shoulder, then down over her breast. "All I want is you, Lora Leigh. And I intend to collect tonight."

She laughed as he rapped on the privacy window separating them from the driver and told him to head to the airport.

But her laughter died as he closed his lips over hers and began to take the pins from her hair. "Just a taste," he whispered against her neck. "One taste to last me until tonight…"

But she knew that one taste would never be enough for either of them.

* * * * *

The suspense and romance of
DIAMONDS AND DADDIES continues next month
with Dana Martin's DESERT ICE DADDY.
Celebrate 60 years of Harlequin Books by not missing
out on this four-book series from Harlequin Intrigue.

Harlequin is 60 years old, and Harlequin Blaze is celebrating!
After all, a lot can happen in 60 years, or 60 minutes...or 60 seconds!
Find out what's going down in Blaze's heart-stopping new miniseries,
FROM 0 TO 60!
Getting from "Hello" to "How was it?" can happen fast....

Here's a sneak peek of the first book,
A LONG, HARD RIDE
by Alison Kent
Available March 2009.

"IS THAT FOR ME?" Trey asked.

Cardin Worth cocked her head to the side and considered how much better the day already seemed. "Good morning to you, too."

When she didn't hold out the second cup of coffee for him to take, he came closer. She sipped from her heavy white mug, hiding her grin and her giddy rush of nerves behind it.

But when he stopped in front of her, she made the mistake of lowering her gaze from his face to the exposed strip of his chest. It was either give him his cup of coffee or bury her nose against him and breathe in. She remembered so clearly how he smelled. How he tasted.

She gave him his coffee.

After taking a quick gulp, he smiled and said, "Good morning, Cardin. I hope the floor wasn't too hard for you."

The hardness of the floor hadn't been the problem. She shook her head. "Are you kidding? I slept like a baby, swaddled in my sleeping bag."

"In my sleeping bag, you mean."

If he wanted to get technical, yeah. "Thanks for the loaner. It made sleeping on the floor almost bearable." As had the warmth of his spooned body, she thought, then quickly changed the subject. "I saw you have a loaf of bread and some eggs. Would you like me to cook breakfast?"

He lowered his coffee mug slowly, his gaze as warm as the sun on her shoulders, as the ceramic heating her hands. "I didn't bring you out here to wait on me."

"You didn't bring me out here at all. I volunteered to come."

"To help me get ready for the race. Not to serve me."

"It's just breakfast, Trey. And coffee." Even if last night it had been more. Even if the way he was looking at her made her want to climb back into that sleeping bag. "I work much better when my stomach's not growling. I thought it might be the same for you."

"It is, but I'll cook. You made the coffee."

"That's because I can't work at all without caffeine."

"If I'd known that, I would've put on a pot as soon I got up."

"What time *did* you get up?" Judging by the sun's position, she swore it couldn't be any later than seven now. And, yeah, they'd agreed to start working at six.

"Maybe four?" he guessed, giving her a lazy smile.

"But it was almost two…" She let the sentence dangle, finishing the thought privately. She was quite sure he knew exactly what time they'd finally fallen asleep after he'd made love to her.

The question facing her now was where did this relationship—if you could even call it *that*—go from here?

* * * * *

Cardin and Trey are about to find out that great sex is only the beginning....
Don't miss the fireworks!
Get ready for
A LONG, HARD RIDE
by Alison Kent.
Available March 2009,
wherever Blaze books are sold.